THE SHORE GHOSTS AND
OTHER STORIES OF NEW JERSEY

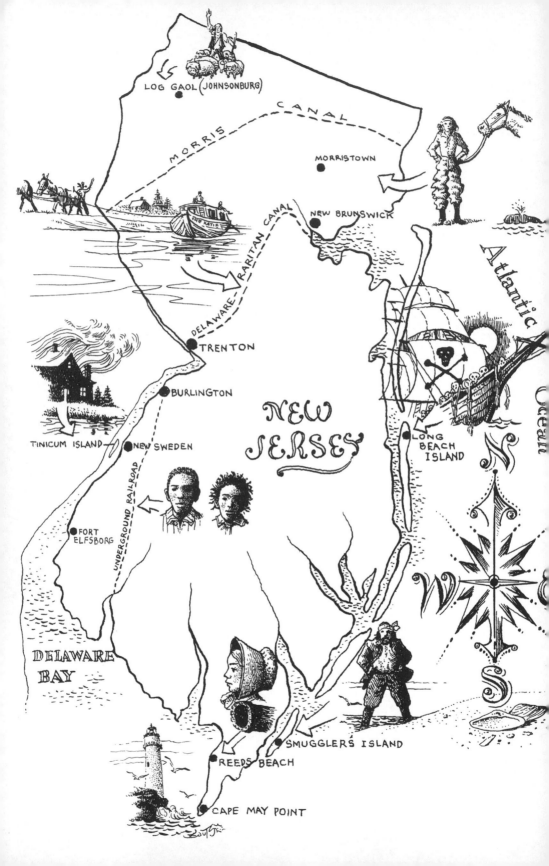

LOG GAOL (JOHNSONBURG)

MORRIS CANAL

MORRISTOWN

NEW BRUNSWICK

THE KATIE

DELAWARE-RARITAN CANAL

TRENTON

BURLINGTON

TINICUM ISLAND

NEW SWEDEN

NEW JERSEY

LONG BEACH ISLAND

Atlantic Ocean

UNDERGROUND RAILROAD

FORT ELFSBORG

DELAWARE BAY

SMUGGLERS ISLAND

REEDS BEACH

CAPE MAY POINT

The Shore Ghosts and Other Stories of New Jersey

BY LARONA HOMER
Illustrated by William Sauts Bock

MIDDLE ATLANTIC PRESS
MOORESTOWN, NJ 08057

Manufactured in the United States of America

Library of Congress Cataloging-in-Publication Data

Homer, Larona C,
    The shore ghosts and other stories of New Jersey.

    Bibliography: p.153
    Contents: The shore ghosts—Journey on the underground railway—A strange guest in the house—(etc.)
    1. Children's stories, American.   (1. New Jersey—Fiction.   2. Short stories)

I. Bock, William Sauts, 1939-   II. Title.
PZ7.H745Sh(Fic)   81-38362
ISBN 0-912608-82-X   AACR2

For information write:
Middle Atlantic Press
10 Twosome Drive
P.O. Box 600
Moorestown, NJ 08057

For all the children
who may read and enjoy these stories

Contents

THE SHORE GHOSTS AND
OTHER STORIES OF NEW JERSEY

The Shore Ghosts

"What kept you so long?" Don asked, as Gerry came up the walk pulling his yellow sweater over his head.

"I had to get my things together so Mom could pack them tonight. She said she wants the station wagon loaded and ready to leave for home by noon tomorrow," Gerry said.

Don knelt down to tie his sneaker, and sighed. "Gosh, I wish summer wasn't over."

"Me too," Gerry agreed. "This time next week we'll be in school."

For nearly three months of the year Don and Gerry were inseparable. Their parents owned summer cottages next to one another on the island. For six years they had come to the sea shore in June and stayed until September.

Many people who vacationed here thought the boys were twins, they looked so much alike. They were both tall for their eleven years. They both had brown eyes that flashed with enthusiasm. They both had unruly blond hair that was bleached almost white by the end of summer.

In the winter it was quite a different matter. Don lived in a community of newly built homes in South Jersey. Gerry lived in North Jersey close to New York City. But even in winter, although they were miles apart, they did practically the same things—scouts, school projects, swimming at the "Y" on Friday evenings, and Little League baseball in the spring.

The real fun, though, was in the summer with its long stretch of warm lazy days, playing ball on the beach, swimming in the ocean, fishing in the bay, exploring.

"Race you to the beach," Gerry said, standing up after he had securely tied both sneakers. But he didn't sound a bit enthusiastic.

"I don't feel like going back to the beach," Don said. Then a bright thought struck him. "Let's go see Mr. Johnson."

"Good idea," Gerry agreed. "We haven't seen him for a long time."

They started down the street.

Mr. Johnson wasn't "summer folks." He was a fisherman who lived alone in a little two room house on the bay. It was so close to his wharf it seemed to be attached to it.

"I don't know how he ever gets through the cold winter months in that flimsy little house," Don's mother often said. "The wind must come in through the cracks and whistle under the doors and windows. Every summer I'm surprised to find him still there."

But every summer Mr. Johnson looked just the same as when they left the year before. He had the same merry twinkle in his clear blue eyes. The same smile creased his weather-lined face with its fringe of whiskers. Only his hair seemed a bit thinner each season.

Mr. Johnson liked the summer people, but he was glad when they went home in the fall and he could be alone with the wind, the water, the gulls—

and the fish. For most of his seventy-five years he had made his living fishing. And for most of that time he had lived in his house on the bay. He said that he would never leave it.

Now he fished just for his own pleasure. He would go out in his little boat no matter how cold it was and catch a few fish for his supper. He never caught more than he could use or give to his friends on the island. Once or twice he had given some to Don and Gerry to take home to their mothers.

The boys came to the end of the paved street and turned down the sandy path through the high grasses that led to Mr. Johnson's house. They found the old fisherman sitting in an ancient rocking chair out on his wharf. A corncob pipe was clenched between his teeth. He wore a faded blue sweater buttoned up the front. A battered sea captain's cap shaded his eyes as he watched the sun setting over the bay. Long rays of red and gold thrust up through the clouds like fingers, and in places the reflection made the water look as though it were on fire. A few boats moved lazily toward their docks. There was an end-of-the-day quiet about everything.

Mr. Johnson looked around as the boys stepped out on his wharf.

"Hello, lads," he said, taking his pipe out of his mouth and pointing with it towards the sunset. "Ever see anything more beautiful? Watch how the colors change as the sun slips down into the water."

Gerry and Don had seen the sun go down hundreds of times, but tonight Mr. Johnson made it seem more special. They stood quietly watching. After the last red lip had disappeared and blue and lavender began to take the place of red and gold, Mr. Johnson turned to the boys.

"Well, show's over. But I never cease to marvel at it," he said. Then, pointing with his pipe to two small crates he had on the wharf he said, "Sit down, lads."

Don and Gerry pulled the crates a little closer to the old fisherman.

"Did you catch any fish today?" Don asked.

"No, didn't go out today," he said, knocking the ashes out of his pipe. "Walked around ocean side this morning; hadn't been there this season. Just wanted to check up on things. See if it looked the same as last time I was there."

"Did it?" Gerry asked.

"Well, yes and no. Sure are a lot more houses than there used to be. Makes me wonder sometimes."

"Wonder what, Mr. Johnson?" Gerry asked.

"Wonder what the people think who settled this island long, long ago."

"When you were a boy?" Don asked.

Mr. Johnson smiled. "No, lad, long before that. Way back when nobody was here but fishermen. Or the folks who was saved when some ship was wrecked off shore. Them few lucky ones still alive when they was washed up, and decided to stay and make their homes here."

"Were there many shipwrecks off this shore?" Gerry asked.

"Why they went down by the dozens out there every year, during bad storms. And warn't but a few on board saved."

"Golly, did you ever see a shipwreck?" Don asked.

"Two of 'em. But most wrecks were before my time. Now there are lighthouses, and radar. But years ago it was bad, real bad. Shipwrecks near all the time, and most everyone on board drowned. Their bodies washed up on shore. And now their ghosts walk the beach on moonlit nights. Been doing it all these many years, they have."

"You mean they still wander up and down the beach?" Gerry asked.

"Yes, poor souls, looking for their friends and family. And they'll walk the beach until they find 'em." He put his pipe in his sweater pocket. "This old beach is full of stories," he said rocking slowly in his chair. "You just go out 'bout midnight when the moon is full and the mist rolls in from the sea. Walk along the water's edge and listen to the voices. Some be laughing, some crying. Others be moaning and wailing. Most of 'em been here on this island for hundreds of years."

"You mean they're ghosts who come back to scare the people who live here?" Gerry asked, his eyes wide with wonder.

Mr. Johnson rubbed his whiskered chin. "No, wouldn't say they come back to scare us. Mostly

they're just poor wanderers looking for loved ones.
There's a few mean ones, though, that's for sure.
Like the pirate from Captain Kidd's gang. He was
killed and buried with the treasure so's his ghost
would protect it from anyone who took the notion
to dig it up. He's real mean, that one is. Chase you
up the beach waving his cutlass. Makes no never-
mind how fast you run, neither, he stays right
behind you. You can hear his footsteps crunching
in the sand. Times he gets so close you can feel his
hot breath on your neck.''

The boys sat on their crates wide eyed, waiting
for Mr. Johnson to continue. After a long pause,
Don asked, ''Did he ever chase you?''

''Nooo,'' he said at last. His forehead was
wrinkled as stories of long ago came tumbling
through his mind. ''Nooo,'' he repeated. ''Can't
say I ever had the misfortune to meet that fellow.''

''Did you ever know anyone who did?'' Don
prodded.

''Yes,'' Mr. Johnson said thoughtfully. ''Friend
of my Pa's, an old fisherman who lived across the
bay. Said he met him face to face. Told me about it
when I was a boy about your size.''

''What did he tell you?'' Gerry whispered.

Mr. Johnson leaned back in his chair and gazed
out at the water in silence for a few moments. Then
he turned to the boys. ''Said it happened one night
in early September, just about this time of year.
There was a full moon. He was walking up the
beach toward his house and he had to pass a tumble

down place along the way—near to where Eighth Avenue is now, as I recollect it. 'Course, there warn't any streets then, just paths of sand between the dunes.

"That old wreck of a house been washed away now. Good sturdy house, too, when it was built. But the storms beat on it year after year, and flood tides got to its foundation so's it tipped starboard and just stayed there—leaning away over at a crazy angle. The windows on one side were buried half way up the sash, it was that crooked.

"Well, as the fisherman passed the house, what do you suppose, but he sees this pale blue light flashing in one of the upstairs windows. There's a sharp wind howling around the house, shutters banging and creaking on their rusty hinges. Then the light leaves the room upstairs and begins to flash pale blue—downstairs."

"Whew!" whispered Gerry.

Don leaned forward and folded his arms across his knees.

"I'll tell you, that man was so frightened he ran as fast as he could past the crooked house. Then footsteps began to follow him. He heard them crunching in the sand. And he felt something between his shoulders, cold as ice.

"He let out an awful howl and turned around. There he was, face to face with the pirate. His eyes gleamed blood red, and his mouth was twisted and ugly. He held his cutlass over his shaggy head, ready to finish the fisherman.

"But he screamed again and ran down the beach."
Mr. Johnson paused.

"Did the pirate catch him?" Don asked.

"Nope. He got home alright and dropped in a
faint right on his porch steps. But when he came
to, he vowed he'd never again walk the beach
alone at midnight, when there was a full moon."
Mr. Johnson was quiet for a moment. "And he
never did," he declared.

"Did anybody ever   see the pirate again?" Gerry
asked.

"Nobody that I know of," Mr. Johnson said.
"Some folks thought maybe he was waiting at the
crooked house for the ghost ship to come get him.
It does come, from time to time."

"A ghost ship here—on our island?" Don questioned.

"Yep," Mr. Johnson said. "Pulls right up here
on the beach. Jim Garrett saw it. Not many folks
believed him, but Jim swears it's true."

"What did Jim—Mr. Garrett—say?" Don asked.

Mr. Johnson reached down in a basket beside
him and took out three large apples. He gave one
to Don and one to Gerry. Then, producing a jack-
knife from his pocket, he began to peel the third one.

"Won't you tell us what Mr. Garrett said about
the ghost ship?" Don repeated taking a bite of
his apple.

Mr. Johnson cut his apple in even size slices.
Popping one in his mouth he half closed his eyes
to get his thoughts in order.

"Jim Garrett likes to fish at night," he began. "One night he was out in his boat alone. Hadn't caught anything. Just seemed the fish warn't biting. Anyway, after a while he beached his boat and started to walk home. There was a full moon. Not a cloud in the sky. As Jim looked out across the water, a mist started to rise. Pretty sight, that is, so he watched it for a time. Then out of the mist, a ship started sailing toward shore, sails full even though there warn't any breeze. Closer and closer it came. Now Jim knows these waters well and saw it was getting too close for safety. He knowed it would run aground if the captain didn't change its tack. But it still kept coming closer. Then Jim realized that this warn't any kind of ship he'd ever seen before. This was one straight out of the past. By now it was so near to him that Jim could make out a skull and crossbones on its sails.

"There right before his eyes it came sailing through the breakers, steady and straight as though it was being towed up on shore. It came in to the shallow water not twenty feet from where Jim was standing.

"But the awful sight was the skeletons hanging from the masthead and leaning over the railings. Nobody was on board. That is, nobody alive. No captain, no crew, no passengers. Only skeletons. Warn't any lights on the ship, but the moon was so bright Jim could see everything on deck just as plain as day."

Mr. Johnson quietly ate another slice of apple.

Don and Gerry sat there in frozen silence, afraid
that if they bit into their apples the snap would
break the spell. At last Don asked, "What happened then?"

Mr. Johnson finished his apple, folded his jack-
knife and put it in his pocket.

"Well, the pirate ship just lay there quiet in the
shallow water. She was waiting for something—or
somebody. When nothing happened, she sailed
away as silent as she sailed in. Nobody got on. Nobody got off. But Jim thought maybe she had come
in to pick up the ghost of a shipmate left behind."

By now it had gotten dark. The sky was full of
stars. Mr. Johnson went inside his house and
lighted his oil lamp—the same one he had when
he built his house over fifty years ago.

The boys sat there quietly, wondering about
the ghosts and the pirate that had lived on their
island, perhaps even right where they lived. They
weren't far from Eighth Avenue.

Mr. Johnson came back and sat in his rocker again.

"I guess we better go," Don said. "Our moms
don't know where we are." But they both sat there.
Then he asked, "Do you believe Jim Garrett's story?"

"Well lad," Mr. Johnson said, slowly rubbing
his chin, "there are many things in this world we
can't explain. And if Jim Garrett says he saw the
phantom ship—well that's good enough for me."

"Do you think sometime we might see the phantom ship or meet the pirate?" he asked timidly.

"Could be. Could be," Mr. Johnson said. He

looked up at the sky full of stars, and the new moon hanging just above his wharf. "But it won't be tonight. So don't be afraid to go home the beach way."

"We're not afraid," Don said, hoping his voice sounded braver than he felt.

"How do you know it won't be tonight?" Gerry asked a bit shakily.

"It takes a full moon, lad. Only happens when the moon is full and a mist rolls in from the sea. That's the kind of night you hear the phantom cries. That's the kind of night the ghost of the black dog gallops up and down the beach."

"The ghost of a black dog?" the boys gasped.

"Yep," Mr. Johnson said. "Gallops up and down, his eyes flaming with fire, the gash in his forehead dripping blood. Keeps his nose down, sniffing the sand, like he's looking for someone."

"Somebody special?" Don whispered.

"Probably his master. The black dog and his master were shipwrecked just off shore during a nor'-easter. The dog was washed up on the beach . . ."

"What happened then?" Gerry asked.

Mr. Johnson yawned. "Well, you come back sometime and I'll tell you that story," he said.

But summer was at an end. The seashore cottages closed for the winter. Don and Gerry went back to school. There hadn't been time to hear about the ghost of the black dog and his master.

Journey on the Underground Railroad

"I don't think we ever find our daddy," Julie said. Tears filled her eyes and spilled over, making little rivers in the dust on her chocolate colored cheeks. "Don't nobody know where we is."

Her brother put his arms around her. "Now Julie, you stop thinkin' that way. Somebody from the Underground Railroad gon' come for us. They sho nuff know we here."

But even as John Henry tried to reassure his sister, he couldn't help wondering if they had been forgotten. Two days had been a long time to hide here in the dusty, hot barn. And now, after eating the last of their hoe cakes and cheese, they were still hungry.

"You make these last," their mamma had said, as she gave John Henry the bag of food.

That was back in Virginia. It seemed so long ago, although it had really only been a few days. Their mamma had been sitting in the rocking chair. There was a far away look in her eyes.

"You 'most twelve year ole, Son, an' you got a big responsibility restin' on yo' shoulders," she had told him. "But they broad shoulders like yo' daddy's. Take care of Julie. I knows you can do it."

"Yes Mamma, I will," John Henry said, hoping she wouldn't see the tears that began to trickle down his black cheeks.

"Mamma, I don't wanna go," Julie sobbed. She

wound her arms around her mother's neck. "Please let me stay here with you!"

Her mother unclasped the little girl's hands and lifted her up on her lap. Gently she rocked back and forth.

"Julie chile, I wish you could." Mamma's voice was soft and low—like when she used to croon to them at bedtime. "But I don't want you an' John Henry taken away an' sold at auction, way yo' daddy an' me was sold. That's what would happen if you stayed here. An' that would break my heart. Cap'n Jamison will take you up to New Jersey on his boat. Then a conductor from the Underground Railroad gon' meet you an' fetch you to yo' daddy. There you be safe from slavery. I be along some day soon, an' we all be together again."

She kissed the top of Julie's head with the tight little pigtails. Then she stood up and gathered John Henry in her arms with Julie. She laid her cool cheek against his hot one.

"How tall you grown, John Henry," she said. "Yo' pant legs don't begin to reach yo' ankles no mo'. You be a big man, like yo' daddy."

Then she released the children. Standing as straight as a poker she asked in a crisp voice, "You sure you knows what to do, John Henry?"

"Yes'm."

"S'pose you tell me again."

John Henry repeated the story. Captain Jamison's schooner THE GRIFFIN would be carrying supplies from Norfolk to Philadelphia. It would stop at

Greenwich, New Jersey to unload barrels of flour. There he and Julie would be taken off the boat by someone who would give them directions for their next stop on their Underground Railroad journey.

"That's right good," their mother said. "Now Julie, you tell me the rest."

"We best be quiet an' always keep outa sight," the little girl said. "We best not speak to nobody 'cept the person singin' the song, 'Sometimes I Feel Like a Motherless Chile.' Then John Henry will answer with the nex' line, 'A long ways from home.' "

"That's right good," her mother said. "An' always remember, it don't make no matter what happen, yo' daddy an' I loves you very much."

Just before midnight an old black man they had never met pulled up to their cabin door with a rickety wagon to take the children to THE GRIFFIN. He shook their mother's hand formally, and smiled kindly at them. His white hair shone silver in the moonlight.

Their mother buttoned Julie's thin cotton jacket and straightened John Henry's shirt. She kissed them and held them very tight for a minute. Then the three of them went out to the wagon and the children climbed in the back. Their mamma was standing very straight and tall as she watched them start off into the misty night. But John Henry knew that she was holding back tears—the same as he was.

He and Julie huddled under a blanket and

bumped along dark narrow roads. When they reached the outskirts of Norfolk, they heard the clop, clop, clop of horse's hooves and the rattle of wagon wheels on the cobbled streets. John Henry figured that they were driven by slaves getting an early start to market, to buy food for families who lived in the big houses near the city.

The old black man stopped the wagon at the wharf where THE GRIFFIN was docked. He let himself down from the seat and threw the blanket off the children.

"We here," he whispered. "Now don't you worry none. We gon' get you to yo' daddy. Come on."

He lifted Julie over the side. John Henry jumped down beside her. They stood in the shadows until a figure appeared on the deck of THE GRIFFIN, swinging a lantern from side to side.

"That's Cap'n Jamison's signal," the old man said. "Go on now." He gently pushed the children toward the gangplank.

They hesitated.

"Go on," he urged.

Slowly they made their way up to the deck. The captain stood at the railing waiting.

"Don't be afraid, children" he said. "I'm going to have to hide you where it's very dark. But you'll be safe. Remember that."

Captain Jamison opened the hatch.

"Follow me," he said, as he climbed down the ladder.

Julie stood frozen, looking into the big, black, bottomless hold of the ship.

"Come on," the captain coaxed. "I won't let you fall."

Slowly the little girl started down the ladder. John Henry followed. By the light of the captain's lantern they could see to follow him to the forward end of the schooner. Here barrels had been stacked high in several rows. Behind them, sacks of grain were piled on one another.

"You'll hide back here," Captain Jamison said, pushing against the sacks so that he made a space between them. "Think you can wiggle through there?" He smiled the kindest smile. "It's going to be tight quarters. You'll have to sit close. But I'm sure brave youngsters like you can make it alright."

The children squeezed in and hunched down in a space not big enough to hold another sack of grain.

"We'll get you out of here as soon as possible," the captain said, pushing the sacks together again.

Through a tiny crack the children watched the little flicker of light as the captain carried the lantern up the ladder to the deck. The hatch cover slid back in place and all was pitch black.

Julie reached for John Henry's hand.

"We safe now," he whispered.

All was quiet in the darkness except for the creaking of the ship's timbers as she gently rolled in her mooring. Then there seemed to be a commotion on deck. Men's voices shouted back and forth, accompanied by the pounding of many feet. The hatch was opened and Captain Jamison came down the ladder followed by a wiry little man wearing a red neckerchief and carrying a crowbar.

The children clung together, every muscle in their bodies bunched in fear.

"You see there's nothing here but my cargo," they heard the captain say, as the two men walked through the hold of the ship. When they came to where Julie and John Henry were hidden he added, "This is flour and grain."

"A good place to hide runaways," the wiry man grunted.

He walked around behind the barrels and pushed against some of the sacks of grain. For a horrible moment, John Henry thought they would tumble over and crush them.

"I'd be glad to open any of them so you can see for yourself," the captain said.

"*I'll* open them," was the answer. Using his crowbar, the man pried the lids off several barrels. At last he called up to the deck, "Nobody's here."

He and the captain climbed the ladder. The hatch was closed. Again it was black as midnight.

"Oh John Henry, I's scared," Julie whispered.

He could feel her trembling. "They gone now," he said softly. But his muscles were in one big knot.

Again all was quiet topside. A short while later THE GRIFFIN set sail from Norfolk.

The children had no idea how long they traveled. They slept off and on, but always when they wakened it was dark. They couldn't tell whether it was night or day. In their cramped little hiding place they nibbled on hoe cakes and cheese, not knowing if they were eating breakfast or dinner.

All of a sudden there were voices calling orders up on deck and THE GRIFFIN bumped something with a muffled thump. The vessel shivered, then it stopped moving. John Henry realized that they were tying up at a wharf. A short while later the hatch was opened. Several men came down into the hold and began carrying the barrels of flour up to the deck.

"They sho' gon' find us now," Julie breathed, holding tight to her brother's hand.

He put his finger over the little girl's mouth. "Sh!"

A voice close to them shouted, "Bring up the sacks too?"

From topside someone answered, "No. They go on to Philadelphia."

"Then that's all here below," the man called, and he bounded up the ladder. The hatch was closed. Once more, darkness.

For a while there wasn't a sound on the ship. It might have been deserted for all they could tell. Then someone slowly opened the hatch and started down the ladder with a lantern. Softly he began to croon, "Sometimes I feel like a motherless chile."

John Henry couldn't find his voice to answer, but Julie did. She sang out, "A long ways from home."

Then a deep voice rumbled, "Come on younguns, we gon' get you off this ship."

The children crept from behind the sacks as a big black man with a warm smile on his face came toward them. "You done had a pretty scarey time down here in the dark, didn't you? Cap'n Jamison say you good sailors. Well, the worst is over now. Let's go topside. Want me to carry you up the ladder, chile?'' he asked Julie.

"No—thank you," she stammered. But she was glad when he lifted her up the last few rungs.

"Now keep close to me," the big man said.

No one else seemed to be on the schooner. Their shadows crept along beside them as they walked across the deck and down the gangplank. They threaded their way through the barrels of flour that had been piled on the wharf, and went down a narrow street where a horse and wagon waited for them. The big man lifted the children in the back of the wagon, and again they were traveling along dark bumpy roads.

It seemed like hours before they came to an old deserted barn.

"You hide here," the man said.

As he pushed open the barn door, moonlight cast a path across the floor making enough light so the three of them could see to climb up to the loft.

"They's sweet smellin' hay here," the big man said. "It make a good soft bed fo' you. An' you be safe as two crickets."

"Will you stay with us?" Julie asked.

"I wish I could, but I gotta help some other black folks on they way to freedom. Soon as it's light, somebody come fo' you. When you hear, 'Sometimes I feel like a motherless chile,' you sing out just like you answered me."

As he left he called up to the loft, "I gotta bolt the barn door on the outside. It's a sign to the next underground conductor that you here."

They heard the bolt slide into place. Again they were alone in the dark except for moonlight shimmering through a small window high up in the peak of the roof. They were so tired as they stretched out on the hay that they were soon sound asleep.

The next thing John Henry knew, a shaft of sunlight was streaming through the little window. He wondered what his mamma was doing now. Probably washing clothes for the missus at the big house. He wondered where his daddy was, and how long it would be before he and Julie were with him. His mamma had told him that the Underground Railroad had taken many slaves to New York and Pennsylvania. Some had even gone to Canada. But their daddy was in Burlington, New Jersey.

Julie was awake now. She was so hungry her stomach rumbled and growled. They ate another hoe cake. Then there were only four left.

"S'pose they don't come fo' us today," Julie said. "S'pose don't nobody know we here an' we starve to death."

"Julie, Mamma would be 'shamed of you if she heard you talk like that," her brother scolded. "You promised her you be brave."

"Well, I ain't brave. I's scared. I wish I was back in Virginia with her," she sobbed.

It was hot and dusty in the loft. Only the continuous buzz of blow flies at the tiny window, and the occasional bird call ouside, broke the quiet.

"Let's see what we can find downstairs," John Henry said.

He started down the ladder. Julie was right behind him. The door was locked on the outside, as the big black man said it would be. There was only one window high up on one wall. It was covered by a shutter hinged on the inside and held closed by a wooden bar. The feed troughs that had once held hay for cattle were filled with cobwebs. A little hay was scattered on the floor of one of the stalls and a rusty pitchfork stood in the corner.

"It look pretty deserted," John Henry said as they climbed back to the loft.

The day dragged by and nobody came for them. John Henry thought he'd better make some plans just in case.

The next morning as it was getting light he crept down the ladder. Taking the pitchfork to the window, he pushed the handle against the bar that held the shutter in place. The bar slipped out of its bracket and fell to the floor. The shutter swung open. He jumped up, grabbed the sill, and chinned himself so he could see out.

A meadow stretched along a thick woods. If no-one came for them today, they could climb out the window and get to the woods. Then—well he didn't know what would happen then, but they couldn't stay here and starve. As he dropped back to the floor he was surprised to see Julie standing by the ladder. He told her his plans.

"You think you can do it if I boost you up, Julie?" he asked.

"I'll try," she answered timidly.

All day they waited, but no one came for them.

Early the next morning John Henry boosted Julie up to the opening. "Now slide around an' face me," he said.

She did as her brother told her.

"Now let yo'self out the window, but hang on with both hands."

She did.

"Now let go an' drop to the ground. It ain't far. I look it all over yesterday."

"I can't. I's too scared," she cried.

"Julie, this ain't no time to be scared. You *can* do it," he shouted angrily. "Hurry up. Let go an' drop!"

She did, and soon John Henry was there beside her. She was so frightened he ached for her. Taking her hand he said softly, "You's a brave girl, Julie. Now we gotta get to the woods. Think you can make it?"

At the edge of the meadow they found a patch of wild strawberries. They tasted so good after all the hoe cakes and cheese, and the children ate until they were stuffed.

They walked through the woods until the sun was high in the sky. Patches of gold splashed on the forest floor where it shone through the trees.

"I sho' thought we come on a path 'fore this," John Henry said.

But the trees became thicker and the bushes seemed to reach out to scratch them.

Julie took her brother's hand. "We lost," she cried. "Oh John Henry, we lost. We never gon' be found. I knows we ain't." She sat down under a tall tree and sobbed.

A grey squirrel on a branch above her wisked his tail. John Henry slid down beside her. "We can't be too far from somewhere," he said. "Somebody sho' find us soon."

"But s'pose it one of them slave hunters." Her tears and sobs were all mixed together.

"The worst they could do is send us back to Virginia. An' you said you wished you was there with Mamma."

"But they might sell us on the auction block!"

"Julie, don't think 'bout that." John Henry spoke quietly, but both of them knew the things that could happen. The slave hunters probably had word already that a boy and girl had left the big house in Norfolk. They would be trying to track them down right now. The children knew, too, that if they were found and sold on the block they might never see their parents or each other again.

Their thoughts were interrupted by a voice far away, singing, "Sometimes I feel like a motherless child." Another voice repeated the words.

"Answer it, John Henry!" Julie urged.

Again they heard, "Sometimes I feel like a motherless child."

And both children sang out as loud as they could, "A long ways from home. A long ways from home!"

The singing kept up. Red squirrels skittered through the woods in front of them as they came closer to each other. Even the birds seemed to be calling, "The children have been found! The children have been found!"

At last they met. A short red haired man with a beard to match, and a freckle faced girl about John Henry's size with long red braids.

"Thee must be Julie and John Henry," the man said, as he brushed aside the last clump of bushes that separated them. "Thee gave Martha and me quite a scare. We went to the barn this morning to fetch thee, and thee weren't there."

"No sir," John Henry said. "We thought we was forgot when nobody came for us for two whole days."

"Forgotten? No lad. Some unfriendly men have been in this area looking for black people. 'Runaway slaves,' they called them. We were afraid to come for thee until the men left. We knew thee were safe in the barn. Thee were told to stay there, were thee not?"

"Yes sir."

"And thee did not do it."

"Don't scold, Father," Martha said. "I would have done the same thing. I think thee very brave, John Henry."

"He sho' is!" Julie piped up.

"Well, we found thee. That's the important thing," the father said. "And we better get home before the woods become dark."

Martha chattered all along the way. The children had never heard anyone say "thee" and "thy" before.

John Henry asked, "Do everybody in New Jersey talk like you?"

Martha laughed. "No. Only those of us who belong to the Society of Friends. We are called Quakers. We have helped many black people escape by the Underground Railroad. But until we found thee, they have all been grown-ups."

"Martha, we could get along faster if thee would stop jabbering," her father scolded. "Tell thy stories when we get home." He started walking so fast the children had a hard time keeping up with him.

It was dusk when they arrived at the big brick farmhouse. Martha's mother was on the porch. A crisp white apron covered her long gray dress. She came down the steps to meet them.

"Thank goodness thee found them, William," she said. Then, putting her arms around the children, "You poor lambs must be so hungry and tired."

That night was one the children would never forget. Never had they seen so much food. They ate chicken and dumplings, fresh peas and apple pie until they couldn't eat another bite. Between mouthfuls they told all that had happened to them.

"I thought we was never gon' be found," John Henry said. "I sho' was scared when we was locked in that barn." He put his hand over his mouth to cover a yawn. "But I guess I was even more scared when we was hid in Cap'n Jamison's boat."

Julie's eyes opened wide in surprise. "I didn't know you was scared!" she exclaimed. "You kept tellin' me to be brave, and I was tryin' to be brave like you."

John Henry laughed. Then Julie laughed. Martha and her parents joined in. Then the mother said, "I'm glad thee still has joy in thy heart after these dreadful days. And it's a stout heart, John Henry, that can give hope and courage to someone else. But now let's get thee a bath and to bed. Thee have had a weary time."

The next day dawned bright and clear. The children were eating their breakfast when someone knocked on the front door.

"That must be the conductor from the Underground Railroad," the mother said, looking at her husband.

"I'll go," Martha said, jumping up from the table.

"Thee sit right here and finish thy breakfast," her father commanded. "I'll have a few words with him." He left the kitchen, closing the door behind him.

From the hall they could hear the men's muffled voices. Martha looked at her mother. The same thought went through both their minds. Had something gone wrong? Would the children be unable to continue their journey?

Then the door opened. A tall black man with sparkling brown eyes and a smile that stretched all the way across his face stepped into the room.

"Daddy!" the children cried, as they slid off their chairs and ran to him.

He picked them both up at the same time. "I found you! I sho' 'nuff found you!" he said, hugging them close.

"Daddy, I thought we never gon' see you again," John Henry said, trying to hold back tears.

But as Julie wrapped her arms around his neck, all she could whisper was "Daddy. My Daddy."

At last he said, "We best be on our way. We got a long ride ahead."

Martha's mother gave them a big hamper of food. "This should last thee the rest of thy journey," she said.

The two men shook hands. After all the goodbyes were exchanged, Julie and John Henry scrambled up on the wagon seat. Their daddy climbed up and sat between them.

Martha reached up and patted Julie's hand. "I hope it won't be long before thy mother is with thee," she said softly.

Julie's eyes misted with tears as she turned to her father. "Daddy, you think Mamma ever gon' be with us again?"

"Sho' she will, Julie. And I have a feelin' it will be real soon." His eyes twinkled with a happy secret as he kissed his little daughter on the nose. Then he gave the reins a flip, and they started toward Burlington.

A Strange Guest in the House

January, 1781 was beginning the same way the old year had ended—cold. Very cold.

Dr. Leddell sat down at the dining room table for a hearty lunch before continuing his rounds to see his sick patients. His wife smiled as she ladled thick vegetable soup from a silver tureen into a bowl.

"Where are the children?" the doctor asked, tucking his napkin under his chin.

"I fed the babies and put them down for their naps," she said.

"And Betsy?' he asked.

"I expect she'll be down in a minute. For the past week she's kept her nose in a book Tempe gave her."

Mrs. Leddell passed the bowl of steaming soup across the table. "This will warm you down to your toes," she said cheerfully. "Cook surely knows what's best on a freezing day like this."

Betsy burst into the room breathless from running down the stairs. "I'm sorry I'm late," she smiled.

Her father and mother both stared at her as she slid into her chair.

A white blouse was tucked inside an oversized pair of her father's old brown riding breeches. The pants knees almost came to the top of her black buttoned shoes. They were gathered at her slim waist and held up with a leather belt. A

41

wide yellow ribbon kept her long brown curls in place.

"Betsy, what ever are you doing in an outfit like that?" her father asked.

"I just wondered if I could have these old breeches." His daughter beamed up at him. "You never wear them, and they'd be great for horse-back riding."

Mother shook her head. "I do declare, I don't know where you get these ideas," she said.

Her father laughed. "Betsy, it really doesn't become a pretty girl like you to dress this way. I think you should learn to ride side-saddle the way the other young ladies of Mendham ride."

"I'm not a young lady yet, Papa. I'm only twelve. But I don't think I'll ever wear one of those horrid serge skirts. Aunt Tempe is a young lady and she doesn't wear one. She wears breeches all the time when she rides."

The doctor smiled as he thought how much his daughter reminded him of Tempe. They even looked alike, and they surely had minds of their own.

"I can keep your breeches, can't I?"

Dr. Leddell was amused. You could never tell what Betsy might ask for next.

"Can't I?" she coaxed.

"I suppose so," he said with a chuckle.

She hopped up from the table and gave him a big hug.

"Betsy, it's awful the way you always get around

your father," Mrs. Leddell said, with a merry twinkle in her eyes. "But why are you dressed this way now?"

"I wondered if I could ride over to see Granny Wick and Aunt Tempe."

"No. Not today. I want you all to stay in the house this afternoon," her father said firmly.

"Why, Papa?"

"There is a rumor that some of General Wayne's troops from the Pennsylvania Line have mutinied at Morristown."

"Mutinied!" mother exclaimed in disbelief. "Not our Continental soldiers!"

"Well you know, my dear, they're having a rough time this winter. Supplies haven't been coming through. Their clothing is threadbare. They're cold and they're hungry. Added to this, they have served their three years as they agreed. Now their time is up. They want their pay and their discharges."

"But mutiny!" Mrs. Leddell exclaimed again. She just wouldn't accept this.

"I heard that a group of soldiers went to General Wayne and informed him that they were going to march to Philadelphia to explain their situation to Congress. The General told them to stay here, that he would speak to Congress. But the soldiers wouldn't listen to him. They threatened to destroy the camp if he didn't let them carry out their plans. A fight broke out. Soldiers on both sides were wounded and a captain was killed.

The Pennsylvania troops won. I heard that they gathered guns from camp and are ready to start back to Philadelphia.''

''But they haven't left yet?'' Mrs. Leddell asked in alarm.

''I'm not sure. But don't you worry my dear. This all happened in Morristown. You and the children are safe here. I'd just feel better if you stayed inside.''

''What about Granny Wick and Aunt Tempe?'' Betsy asked.

''I'm sure they'll be all right too. These soldiers aren't out to harm anyone. They just want to go home. Perhaps I'll have more news when I return at dinner time.''

He folded his napkin and excused himself from the table. He looked at Betsy and shook his head. ''I never thought my pants would come to this!'' he grinned.

''Well Aunt Tempe wears riding breeches,'' she said again.

''But hers fit,'' he chortled, as he left the room.

Betsy loved her Aunt Tempe. Aunt Tempe had taught her to ride when she was still so small she had to be lifted into the saddle. ''Some day you'll have your own horse,'' she'd told Betsy. ''And she'll be beautiful. Just as beautiful as Nutmeg.''

Nutmeg was a soft velvety brown with a black mane and tail. She held her head high and looked at you with intelligent brown eyes. Aunt Tempe said that she was an aristocrat. And she was so gentle.

Now Betsy had her own horse, Lady. She loved to ride the mare over to the Wick farm and go for a gallop with her aunt and Nutmeg. She had hoped to do this today, but Papa had changed her plans.

A knock on the front door interrupted her thoughts.

"I'll see who it is, Mama," she said, jumping up from the table and running to open it.

There stood Aunt Tempe wrapped in a heavy cloak and showing beneath it were her riding breeches.

"Oh Aunt Tempe, come in," Betsy said, giving her favorite aunt a big hug.

"What are you doing in your father's breeches?" Tempe asked, holding her niece at arm's length to look at her.

"Papa's giving them to me—for riding," Betsy giggled. "Don't they look neat?"

Tempe laughed. "They're gorgeous. And there's plenty of room for you to grow."

Mrs. Leddell came from the dining room. "Tempe, what ever brings you out on such a bitter cold day?" she asked.

Tempe's nose and cheeks were almost as red as the scarf she had bundled around her neck.

"Probably Nutmeg wanted some exercise," the doctor joked as he came down the hall wearing his great coat.

"Well it is nippy," Tempe said, "but my real reason for coming is to get some medicine for Mama. She's having those headaches again."

"Oh dear. Do you think the doctor should see her?" Mrs. Leddell asked.

"No, I'm sure it's nothing serious. You know she gets them every so often."

"Let me give you something for them," the doctor said. He opened his bag, shook some little pink pills in an envelope and handed them to her.

"Tempe, did you see any soldiers on the road?" her sister asked.

"Soldiers? No, why?" Tempe questioned.

Betsy was anxious to tell the news about the mutiny. "I wanted to ride Lady out to the farm this afternoon, but at lunch Papa told us. . ."

"I told you it was too cold to go," he said, not wanting to alarm his sister-in-law. "Now Tempe, why don't you take off your cloak and visit for a while?"

"No thank you. I had better get back and give Mama her medicine."

Tempe kissed her sister and her neice. She shook hands with her brother-in-law.

"I'll ride out tomorrow just to make sure everything is all right," he said.

"I'll come too," Betsy called as Tempe went down the walk to the gate where Nutmeg was waiting.

"I must be on my way," the doctor said, kissing his wife and daughter. "Now don't worry. Not even about Tempe. She can take care of herself." He picked up his bag and followed her down to the gate where his own horse was tethered.

Patches of snow still clung to the edges of Jockey Hollow Road as Tempe and Nutmeg galloped home. She leaned forward and patted the mare's sleek neck. "We don't mind the cold, do we?" she whispered.

They came to the rise that marked the halfway point between Mendham and the Wick farm when suddenly four men appeared from behind the trees just ahead and came striding toward her. They wouldn't budge to let her pass. She brought Nutmeg to a halt so she wouldn't run them down. For a moment she was frightened. Then she realized that these were Continental soldiers, some of General Washington's army. They wouldn't harm her.

One of the soldiers smiled up at her and took hold of the bridle. "It's a beautiful horse you have," he said.

"Yes," Tempe agreed. "She's smart too."

The others walked around Nutmeg patting her flanks and admiring her shiny coat.

Tempe heard the tall yellow haired soldier ask, "Who's the girl?"

"She's from the Wick farm two miles down the road," his comrade answered. "I've seen her ride through here before."

"So have I," the yellow haired one answered, "but I never knew where she came from. She sure has a nice looking horse."

"What do you think?" the fourth soldier asked the one who was holding the bridle.

"I think we better take her," he answered.

"What do you mean, 'take her'?" Tempe asked in surprise.

"Take your horse," the soldier replied. His grey

eyes made Tempe think of the ice on the puddles in the road. "We can use a good mare. We have quite a trip ahead of us."

"Where are you going?" she demanded.

"To Philadelphia as soon as we have transportation."

"You mean General Wayne is moving his troops out of Morristown?"

"Oh no. *He's* staying," the yellow haired one laughed. "Now if you'll get down off your horse. . ."

"Stop ordering me around," Tempe said angrily. "Nutmeg and I aren't in the army."

"Let's stop this talking and get on our way," one of the men snapped. "Take the horse. The girl doesn't live far from here. She can walk home."

"Come on, miss," the first soldier said, dropping the reins to help her dismount.

With that, Tempe gave Nutmeg a sharp slap with her crop. The mare dashed away from the startled soldiers. It was a few seconds before they realized what had happened. Then they started after her, running and firing musket shots in the air. Tempe's heart was beating faster than Nutmeg's hoofs were flying.

As they sped over the ground Tempe wondered what she would do when they arrived home. The soldiers knew where she lived. They would surely follow her and take Nutmeg from the barn. Then a thought flashed through her mind.

Instead of going to the barn she rode straight to the front gate. It was open. They went through.

She slid from the saddle and latched the gate behind her. Firmly holding the bridle she led Nutmeg
up the front walk, around the path at the side and
on to the back of the house. Urging the mare up the
steps she opened the back door and led her through
the kitchen, through the hall with its highly
polished floor, through the parlor with the rose
flowered carpet, and into the guest room behind
the parlor.

Mrs. Wick was lying down in her bedroom. She
listened as the back door opened and closed. Then
she thought her ears must be deceiving her. They
couldn't be horse's hoofs she heard clopping
through the hallway! She slipped out of bed and
hurried downstairs. She went into the parlor. Then
into the guest room.

"TEMPERANCE!" she exclaimed, hardly believ-
ing what she saw. "What on earth. . ."

"It's all right, Mama," Tempe started to explain.
Her eyes were so filled with angry tears she could
hardly see to remove Nutmeg's saddle. "It's all
right, really! I'll take care of Nutmeg and feed her
and clean up and—oh, Mama. . ." She put her
arms around her bewildered mother and told her
briefly what had happened.

"The only place she'll be safe is here in the
house. We've got to let Nutmeg stay here until the
soldiers leave."

She peeked through the slats of the closed shutters. "See, Mama, they're here already."

Her mother looked. The soldiers were running

down the road. When they reached the barn, two of them went inside. The other two searched the out-buildings. They even looked in the chicken coops.

"Now really, you don't suppose they expected to find Nutmeg there," Tempe said with a smirk.

Mother didn't smile. She could see nothing amusing about this situation. In fact she couldn't even believe what she was seeing . . . until she noticed Nutmeg's saddle on her beautiful hand-made bedspread!

"Temperance, look what you've done!" she cried.

"Oh Mama, I *am* sorry." She lifted the saddle off the bed and stood it in the corner. "We better take the spread off," she said. Carefully folding it she put it in the parlor. Then she looked around the guest room. "Let's put these chairs in the parlor too," she added.

Mrs. Wick watched helplessly as her daughter rearranged the room. Nutmeg looked on quietly, only occasionally pawing the polished floor.

Through the shutters they saw two of the soldiers walking down the road. The other two were sitting on the fence, apparently expecting Tempe and Nutmeg to arrive at any time.

They were still sitting there when the sun went down.

Tempe couldn't go to the barn to get hay or oats for her horse. Not while the soldiers were there. If Mama went for it they would suspect something very strange was going on. The best thing for all of them to do was to keep out of sight. Nutmeg would have to eat people food for her supper.

Tempe brought her some bread and an apple.

"Poor Nutmeg," she said, putting her cheek against the horse's face.

"Poor Nutmeg, humph!" Mrs. Wick declared. "Poor me! Never before did I hear of a horse spending the night in a beautiful guest room. Tomorrow Temperance, no matter what, you'll have to take her to the barn." Mrs. Wick had a determined look as Tempe closed the guest room door and went up to her bedroom.

Early the next morning she looked out her window. No-one was to be seen. She breathed a sigh of relief. Quickly she dressed, stole out the back door and ran across the lawn. Cautiously she peeked in the barn, almost expecting to see a soldier asleep in Nutmeg's stall. But the barn was empty.

She gathered an armful of hay. Then she thought, suppose the soldiers come back. She might not be able to come to the barn again. She'd better take a whole bale while she had the opportunity.

She was dragging the bundle of hay through the hall when her mother met her at the foot of the stairs.

"Temperance, I'll never get over this," she said tying her apron around her waist. "Just look at what you're doing to these beautiful floors."

"I know, Mama. Believe me I'm sorry. I'll polish them again. But Nutmeg must have something to eat." She continued to drag the bale across the rose flowered carpet.

As she opened the guest room door, Nutmeg whinnied softly and clumped across the floor to greet her.

"I don't know how long you'll have to stay here," Tempe said patting her nose. "So please behave yourself. Mama doesn't understand."

Then an awful thought struck her. The medicine! She hadn't given her mother the medicine! How could she have been so thoughtless? And her mother hadn't said a word about it.

"Mama," she called as she hurried to the kitchen. "How are you? I feel so terrible. I'm such a dreadfully selfish person. I was only thinking of Nutmeg. I never gave you the pills."

"It's all right Temperance. I feel as chipper as a cricket this morning. With all the confusion yesterday there wasn't time to think about a headache. I guess Nutmeg was the best medicine for me."

"Oh Mama, you're great." Tempe put her arms around her mother's slim waist and twirled her around the kitchen. They were both laughing when a knock on the front door surprised them.

"It must be the soldiers!" Mrs. Wick exclaimed in alarm.

"I'll go," Tempe said a bit fearfully.

What a delightful surprise it was to find Dr. Leddell and Betsy standing there.

"I thought I'd better check on Mother Wick," the doctor said. "How is she this morning?"

"I'm fine, thank you," Mrs. Wick said coming in

from the kitchen. "Though I can't understand why, with such strange things happening." She shook hands with her son-in-law and hugged her granddaughter. "Take off your cloaks and we'll tell you all about it."

They had just seated themselves at the dining room table when they heard a low neighing. Then, with all the dignity of a royal guest, Nutmeg appeared in the doorway.

"What's this?" the doctor asked in amazement.

"Oh Temperance, you forgot to close the guest room door!" Mrs. Wick exclaimed.

"The guest room door?" the doctor laughed. "How long has Nutmeg been occupying your guest room?"

"That's what I want to tell you about," she said. Then looking at Tempe she added, "Quickly get your horse back there."

Tempe led the confused Nutmeg across the hall, through the parlor and back to her elegant quarters. Then, over cups of tea, she told Betsy and her father what had happened after she had left them the day before.

They laughed when she got to the part about bringing the horse into the house.

"It isn't funny," sighed Mrs. Wick. "I'm afraid my beautiful home will never be the same."

"Yes it will, Granny Wick," Betsy said. "I'll help Aunt Tempe straighten up. We'll fix everything as bright and shiny as new."

"And you can start right now," her father said.

"You needn't worry any longer. The Pennsylvania troops are on their way to appeal to Congress. And here in Morristown, General Wayne is in command again. Nutmeg can go back to her stall in the barn."

"Suppose she likes it here and wants to live in your house, Granny?" Betsy asked impishly.

"Heaven forbid!" her grandmother exclaimed, closing her eyes as if to shut out the horrible thought.

Betsy scooted over and put her arm around her. "Anyway, Granny Wick, I'll bet you're the only person in New Jersey who ever had a horse stay in her guest room overnight."

"I'm sure she is," Tempe agreed.

"Maybe the only one in the whole country," Betsy added.

Smuggler's Island

Jeff knelt on the dock cleaning the blue fish he had just caught for his mother. As he put the last one in the basket he said, "Well Ladd, that should be enough for dinner."

The collie was stretched out on the dock watching the hungry gulls coasting in the air just above them, waiting patiently for the parts of fish that had been discarded. He wagged his tail when he heard his name.

Jeff stood up, wiped his hands on his faded overalls and pushed the old sea captain's cap to the back of his head. Then he picked up his gear and the basket of fish, and started home. Ladd trotted along beside him.

As he strode up the road, Jeff saw Sheriff Swain's horse standing beside his fence. Inside the gate the sheriff and his father were in serious conversation.

When Jeff was close enough, he heard the sheriff say, "Of course, we're only making a routine check. I'm sorry we had to bother you, Mr. Jennings. Thanks for your help." Then he noticed Jeff with his basket of fish. "Hello, boy," he said, a smile replacing his worried frown. "The blues biting today?"

"Yes sir," Jeff answered.

The sheriff swung up into his saddle and was off.

"What was that all about?" A puzzled look wrinkled Jeff's sun tanned face.

"Well son, seems there's been quite a bit of smuggling going on." Mr. Jennings knocked his pipe against the gate post. Dead ashes fell to the ground. "Coast Guard's traced it to this area," he said.

"They don't think that *we're* smugglers, do they?" Jeff gasped.

"Course not," his father chuckled. "But they want us to keep a weather eye out in case we see or hear anything suspicious. If we do, we're to get in touch with the sheriff or Captain Hughes of the Coast Guard immediately."

Pointing at the basket of fish, he smiled. "Looks like a good dinner. Better get them to your mother. She's waiting to fry them."

Mr. Jennings put his arm around his son's shoulders and they went around to the back of the house. Ladd nosed in between them.

"Don't let's say anything about smugglers at dinner," Father cautioned. "Best not to worry your mother or Jenny."

Mother met them at the door wearing the big blue apron she always wore when she fried fish. It reached from just under her chin all the way down to her shoe tops.

"Oh Jeff, what a beautiful catch," she said, taking the basket from him. Her green eyes were glinting with little flecks of gold, the way they always did when she was pleased. "And how nicely you've cleaned them. I think you're the best fisherman on the bay." She brushed his cheek with a kiss.

Jeff smiled. His mother had a way of making him and Jenny feel so important.

Then she gave Mr. Jennings that same kind of

brush-your-cheek kiss. "The pan's ready. By the time you two have washed up, the fish will be cooked. So hurry!"

At dinner Jeff found it hard not to ask questions about the smugglers. He didn't even have a chance later that evening to talk to his father alone. He went to bed with a dozen different thoughts racing through his head.

He wondered if Cap'n Hawkeye, who had moved into the deserted house, could be one of the smugglers. He looked as if he might be. "But I shouldn't say that," Jeff thought. "Pa said you should never judge a man by appearances."

Jeff had first met the captain one drizzly day about two weeks ago. It had been too wet to help his father in the field, so he decided to go down to the marshes to see how the marsh birds had grown. He whistled for Ladd, but the collie was off exploring somewhere, so he went on alone.

Before he realized it, he had wandered further down the road than he usually did, to a place where it turned off on an overgrown path. If you went one way, the path led to a deserted house. The other way took you to a rickety old dock where you could see across the sound to the southern tip of the island.

Jeff took the path to the dock. As he got close he was surprised to see that it had been shored up, and the rotted timbers all replaced with good boards. It was as solid as new. And there at the side, a rowboat was securely tied.

He walked up the path from the dock to the

house, now almost hidden by oaks and sweet
gums. It looked empty and forlorn. Not far from
the porch he found fresh wagon tracks in the soft
sand. This seemed strange. Who would bring a
wagon in to this deserted place? Cautiously he
stole through the tall grass and weeds to the other
side of the house and peeked in the window.

All at once he was grabbed by the collar of his
slicker and practically lifted off his feet.

"What'cha doin' here, boy?" a gravelly voice
rasped in Jeff's ear.

Frightened nearly out of his skin, Jeff twisted
around and looked up into the ugly face of a
man with a big black walrus mustache. A red
bandana was tied around his long stringy hair. He
kept his right eye closed and stared at Jeff with the
other one.

"I ought to slit your gizzard," he said, putting
his bristled cheek right close to Jeff's smooth one.
Then he pulled a knife from his belt. "Or maybe I
ought to cut off your ears," and he touched Jeff's
ear with the cold blade.

A shiver ran down Jeff's spine. His heart was
beating so fast he thought it would jump right out
of his slicker.

Then the man set Jeff down on the ground with a
jolt. "Now get off'n Cap'n Hawkeye's property,"
he boomed. "And if'n you dare to trespass again,
I'll carve you up in little pieces for the gulls to
make a meal of you." He waved the knife in front
of Jeff's face.

"Y-y-yes sir," Jeff stammered and he raced, stumbling, through the overgrown path to the road. Here the ground was smoother and he ran as fast as he could until he was some distance away. When he was sure he wasn't being followed, he stopped for a few minutes to catch his breath, then he hurried home. Ladd was in the yard waiting for him.

"Fine friend you are," Jeff grumbled as the collie bounded to him. "Where were you when Cap'n Hawkeye was about to slit my gizzard?" Ladd licked Jeff's hand and the two of them sat down on the front steps in the drizzle. Jeff had some thinking to do. He decided he'd better not tell his pa about this afternoon. He'd surely be scolded for trespassing. Besides, his mother had told him to keep away from the deserted house.

The next few days Jeff's thoughts were filled with the one-eyed captain. He wondered if he always carried that long knife in his belt. And why wasn't he sailing a ship now if he were a real captain? And what was in the deserted house that he didn't want Jeff to see?

The days passed into weeks. Jeff was so busy helping his pa in the fields that thoughts of the captain began to fade from his mind.

One sparkling clear morning just a whisper of a breeze blew through the cottage door. While he was eating his breakfast his mother said, "Jeff, would you row over to the island and gather some beach plums? Jenny and I will make jelly tomorrow. Your father said that he won't need you in the field today."

"Sure," Jeff said, swallowing his last mouthful of pancakes.

"May I go with him?" his sister asked.

"Not this time, Jenny dear. We must do the baking today."

Jeff sighed a sigh of relief. Sure, for a ten-year-old girl Jenny was fun to be with. But she didn't like to explore the way he and Ladd did. She'd want to come home as soon as they had gotten their beach plums.

As Jeff stepped out of the house the collie ran up to him.

"Want to go over to the island, boy?" he asked.

The dog wagged his tail and started down to the wharf. Jeff picked up two buckets and followed.

"How bout some lunch?" Jenny called, running after him. She stuffed a bag of sandwiches into one of the buckets. "I wish I could go with you," she sighed. "It would be much more fun than baking bread."

It made Jeff feel a bit guilty when he saw how disappointed she was. "I'll take you next week if Pa doesn't need me in the field," he said gruffly, pushing his skiff into the bay.

Instead of hoisting the sail he decided to row to the island. It was only a mile away. Ladd was already sitting in the bow, as much a part of the little boat as the figure-head on one of the pirate ships Jeff liked to read about.

The sun shone golden on the water where the breeze made little ripples. Jeff took off his shirt and stuffed it in the bucket with his lunch.

When they reached the island, he slipped over the side of the boat and pulled it up at his favorite mooring place. Ladd jumped out with a splash. Ahead of them were the dunes, where over the years the wind had blown the sand into high mounds. Tall grasses waved across them and twisted old cedar trees leaned close to the ground.

From the top of the dunes they could look out across the Atlantic Ocean. Today it was almost as calm as the bay. Little waves broke lazily on the beach, leaving a fringe of white foam on the sand.

They walked along the water's edge for a while. Then Jeff said, "Let's take a swim, Ladd. The beach plums can wait till later."

He pulled off his overalls, threw them on the sand and dove into the surf. As he swam through the bracing water and tasted the salt on his lips, he thought that he liked this ocean more than anything in the world. Ladd liked it too. He would go out of the water several times to shake himself, then he'd race right back in again, swimming through the breakers with Jeff.

It must have been noon when they stretched out on the warm sand to dry off. Jeff put on his pants and shirt and shared his lunch with Ladd.

"Well boy, we better pick those beach plums," he said at last. "After all, that's what we were sent here for."

A large patch of fruit grew not far away and it
didn't take long to fill his buckets. He looked
around for Ladd. The collie was back at the water's
edge, half buried in a hole he was digging. Sand was
flying. But a whistle soon brought the dog running.

"Ready for a walk down the beach?" Jeff asked.
"We'll leave the beach plums here and pick them
up on the way back."

Ladd gave happy little yips and started leading
the way. They walked several miles to the end of
the island. Here the shoreline jutted into a point,
and the ocean met the inlet and bay. As they went
around the point to the bay side, something between two of the dunes caught Jeff's attention. It
looked like the square sail of an abandoned ship
slowly waving back and forth. Ladd saw it too. He
growled deep in his throat.

"Now what do you suppose it could be? It wasn't
here the last time we came to the island," Jeff said.

Ladd started towards it.

"No boy. Stay," Jeff commanded.

Keeping close to each other they inched along
the edge of the dunes until they were close enough
to tell what it was.

"It's a lean-to," Jeff whispered. "Now who would
build a shack like that in this place? And what
would it be for?"

Three sides and the roof were made of old
weathered boards. A ragged sail covered the fourth
side. This was nailed to the roof and anchored at
the bottom by piles of sand along the edge. But the

wind had blown much of the sand away and the
sail was free to flap in the breeze.

They plodded up to the shack. Jeff lifted a corner
of the sail. It was too dark to tell what was inside.
He lifted it higher and crept in. He could see piled
against the back of the lean-to, a dozen or more burlap sacks, all stamped with the words, SUGAR—
PUERTO RICO. Beside them stood several crates.
Each one was almost big enough to make a
dog house for Ladd. SMUGGLER'S ISLAND was
scrawled on each box in uneven lettering.

"Well I'll be," Jeff said in a whisper. "So this is
where the smugglers store their stuff."

Ladd bounded into the lean-to and tugged at
Jeff's pant leg.

"What is it, boy?"

The dog whined, pulling Jeff to the opening.

Outside Ladd stood rigid, looking up the shore
line on the bay side of the island. Not far away, a
man was pulling a sledge over the firm beach close
to the water's edge. Around his head was a
red bandana.

"It's Cap'n Hawkeye!" Jeff gasped. Quickly he
pulled the canvas back in place. "Come on Ladd,"
he whispered. "And be quiet."

They crept through the dune grass to where it
was tall and thick enough to hide them. Here they
could keep an eye on the captain without being
seen. They watched him come closer. When he
was opposite the lean-to, he left the sledge and
plowed through the soft dry sand, up to the shack.

Right away he saw the loose end of the canvas flapping in the breeze. He turned and looked up and down the beach.

"I hope he doesn't see our footprints," Jeff whispered.

Then the captain looked towards the dunes.

What if the grass didn't hide them? What if Hawkeye found them? They'd probably both have their gizzards slit! Jeff's heart began to thump. He stretched out flat. Ladd flattened out too, with his chin on his paws. After what seemed like hours, Jeff raised himself a little bit on one elbow.

He saw the captain tumbling one of the crates end over end through the soft sand. When he reached the sledge, he let the crate drop on it with a thud and started back to the lean-to.

"Get down again!" Jeff pushed Ladd's head into the grass.

Now Hawkeye dragged two sacks of sugar from the shack and lifted them up on top of the crate. He pulled and tugged until he got the sledge slowly moving. He didn't have to drag it very far. His rowboat was a short distance up the beach in a cove. Jeff and Ladd watched as he transferred the unwieldy cargo to the tiny craft.

The boat tipped and rocked and looked as though it would surely upset. But Hawkeye finally managed to get it loaded and everything tied in place. He hid the sledge in the marsh grass and rowed across the sound to the dock at the deserted house.

"So that's why he didn't want me on his property," Jeff said, as a grin spread over his face. "He didn't want me to see the stuff he's been smuggling." He stood up and stretched. Suddenly he realized it must be getting late. His mother would begin to worry about him.

"Come on Ladd, we better be going," he said, and started jogging down the beach to where he had left the beach plums. By the time they reached the skiff, a stiff breeze had come up. Jeff raised the sail. Soon they were moving fast across the bay.

Now Jeff knew that Cap'n Hawkeye was the smuggler. No doubt about it. He wondered whether he should tell his father or go right to Sheriff Swain.

He didn't have to wonder long, for when he reached his landing the sheriff was standing there.

"Hello Jeff," he said as the boy tied up his skiff and furled the sail. "Been over to the island, I see."

"Yes sir. Ma wanted beach plums for jelly."

"See any strangers over that way?"

Then Jeff took a big deep breath, slowly exhaled, and began to tell the sheriff his story. He started with his meeting Cap'n Hawkeye at the deserted house two weeks ago. He told him how the dock had been repaired. He told about the lean-to at the tip of the island and what was in it. He told how he and Ladd had watched the captain haul a crate and two sacks of sugar down the beach on a sledge, put them in his boat and row across the sound to the deserted house.

"Hmm." Sheriff Swain frowned as he listened. At last he said, "Jeff, you've just found the link we need to put this rascal in jail. Come on, we'll go find Captain Hughes. I want him to hear your story."

"Yes sir," Jeff agreed. "But could I please take these beach plums to Ma first? I've been gone since breakfast. She'll wonder what happened to me."

The sheriff smiled. "Of course," he said. "But don't be long. I'll wait right here for you."

From then on, things happened so quickly they made Jeff's heart pound. First they got in Sheriff Swain's fast boat and sailed up the water-way to Corson's Inlet where the coast guard cutter, SHOOTING STAR was tied up. The sheriff and Jeff went on board. Captain Hughes was getting ready to cast off for shore patrol, but he listened attentively as Jeff repeated his story.

"Good boy, Jeff," the captain said when he had finished. "You've given us just the information we need. For quite a while we've suspected that Hawkeye was in on this business. But we had no real proof. We knew that smugglers were landing sugar and leather somewhere along the coast and that it was being picked up and taken to Philadelphia. But we couldn't find out where the smugglers put it ashore or how it got inland. Now it's all as clear as day. They stored it in the lean-to, Hawkeye transferred it to the deserted house, and a wagon picked it up there."

"I don't understand why we couldn't see that lean-to from the mainland," the sheriff said frowning.

"He had it too carefully hidden between those

two dunes," Captain Hughes explained. "We couldn't see it from the ocean either."

"Probably even Ladd and I wouldn't have seen it if that old sail had been fastened down tight," Jeff added.

"Well Jeff, now that you've found the hiding place, we'll move in tonight and take care of the rest," the captain said. "We sure do appreciate the information you've given us. This might have gone on for a long time if you hadn't discovered Hawkeye's lean-to."

A smile creased the captain's weather lined face. He reached to his own chest, unfastened the gold Coast Guard insignia sparkling in the sun's rays, and pinned it on Jeff's shirt. Then stepping back, he saluted Jeff. "Thank you, sir," he said to the boy.

Jeff stood as tall as he could stretch and returned the salute. "Yes sir," he said. "Thank you, sir."

Jeff was quiet as he and the sheriff sailed back to Jennings' landing. Ladd was patiently waiting there for him. As Jeff climbed out of the boat the sheriff said, "Thanks again, son." Then he turned his craft around and headed for his own wharf.

Jeff knelt down beside Ladd and put his arm around the collie's neck. "Maybe someday I'll be the captain of a coast guard cutter like SHOOTING STAR," he whispered, as he stroked the soft fur under Ladd's chin. His other hand he put over his gold medal.

The Fire at Printzhof

"Get up Lars," Mother called from the kitchen. "I want you to catch some fish for breakfast."

Lars uncurled on his mattress in the loft. The sun was already pushing through the tiny cracks in the cabin wall where the logs had separated as they dried out. His father had told him to fill up those chinks with mud. Well, he would do it this week. But it was good to feel the spring breeze blow through them, cooling his face.

He stretched and yawned.

"Lars, are you dressing?" his mother called again.

"Here I come," he answered, hopping off the bed.

He pulled on his leather breeches, ran his fingers through his thick yellow hair and climbed down the ladder to the kitchen. His mother and sister were preparing maize cakes.

Lars dipped his finger in the bowl of sweet batter and licked it:

"What a lazy boy you are," his mother scolded. Then she smiled and patted his cheek, leaving a smudge of corn flour on it. "Your father has been working in the field since dawn. He'll be in for breakfast soon, and he'll be hungry as a bear. You know how he enjoys fish in the morning. It shouldn't take you long to catch a few."

"I enjoy them too, and I'm hungry as a little bear," his sister said as she spooned the batter into the iron pan. "Catch a fish for me."

"I'll catch two of them for you, Ingrid," Lars
teased, and gave her blonde braids a gentle tug as
he went past her.

He got his oars and net from the woodshed and
ran down the path to the water's edge. He put them
in the dugout, untied the rope that fastened the
little boat to the dock, and pushed out into the
clear cold water of the South River. It was a good
season for fish. Shad and sturgeon were running
in great schools. He rowed a short distance from
shore and cast his net. This wasn't as much fun as
fishing with a line, but it was quicker. In no time
he had more than enough shad for their breakfast.

The sun felt warm as he rowed back to shore. It
promised to be a good day. He whistled a tuneless
little whistle while he gutted the plump fish and
strung them on a piece of marsh grass.

He could smell the hot fat sputtering in the
skillet when he came into the kitchen.

"Thank you, Lars," his mother said as she took
the fish from him. "They look so good. I know your
father will like them."

"So will I," Ingrid added.

"They'll be ready in a jiffy, Sven," Mother called over her shoulder.

Mr. Svensen had already started his breakfast,
and a bowl of porridge and a pitcher of goat's milk
was at Lars' place across the table from him.

"Good morning, son," he greeted Lars. "I didn't
expect fish for breakfast today. It was so late when
you got to bed last night that I thought you'd sleep

a while longer this morning." Even though Mr. Svensen's blue eyes had a merry twinkle, there was a serious tone in his deep voice. "What did you think of the meeting last night?" he asked.

"It was good I guess," Lars said with a bit of a frown crossing his face. "But why does Governor Printz want to build a fort here at New Sweden?"

"To protect us against the English and Dutch. You heard the governor say that."

"But we already have Fort Christina. Why do we need *another* one? I thought the English and Dutch were going to be our friends," Lars said, still frowning.

"I thought so too, Sven," Mother said.

"We are hoping that will be," Father replied. "But as soon as Governor Stuyvesant arrived in New Amsterdam from Holland, *he* built a fort. And the English have forts up and down the river. If we build Fort Elfsborg down the river, it will be added protection. Governor Printz knows what he's doing. He's a wise man."

"He's a *big* man," Ingrid said, bringing the platter of maize cakes to the table. "I heard Nils Jacobsen say that he weighs four hundred pounds and is almost seven feet tall. He calls him 'Printz the Tub!' "

Lars chuckled. "The Indians call him 'Big Belly,' " he said. Ingrid giggled so hard that the platter she was holding tilted all the way forward, and two maize cakes landed on the table, directly in front of her father.

"Enough of that, both of you," Father scolded. "Johan Printz is the Governor of New Sweden and we will respect him. He governs well. And that's important."

"Well, I hope we can live here in peace. There is plenty of rich land and good water for everyone," Mother sighed.

As they finished their breakfast Father said, "Lars, last night I promised Bjorn some watermelon seeds. Will you take them to him this morning? It's time they were planted."

"I don't know who he is."

"Sure you do. He's one of Governor Printz's farm hands. He sat behind us at the meeting. Row over to Tinicum Island. You'll find him somewhere behind PRINTZHOF working in the field."

Tinicum Island was in the South River halfway between New Sweden on the east, and Fort Christina on the west. PRINTZHOF was the home the governor had built there for his wife and five daughters. Father said it was built of hewn logs. It was much larger than any other home in New Sweden, and it had real glass windows and many brick fireplaces. On one side was a chapel. On the other side was a room built for taking a steam bath. It was called a sauna.

Lars remembered the sauna they had in Sweden. Benches were built around the walls, and a large pile of stones was laid in the middle of the room. You made a fire under the stones. When they became really hot, you sprinkled them with water.

The water hissed and turned into steam. You kept this up until the room was filled with a sweltering cloud. You sat on the benches until you were hot and sweaty. Then you gently brushed yourself with birch switches. This made the blood pump through your body fast and you tingled all over. Father said that this was the best kind of bath to take, and that some day they'd have a sauna in New Sweden.

Lars was thinking how great this would be when his father interrupted his thoughts. "Here Lars, these are the seeds for Bjorn. Don't lose any of them. Tell him to plant them where they'll get lots of sun."

As Lars started down the path to the river, his father called, "I'll need you to help me in the field today. Don't be too long."

Lars pushed the dugout into the water and rowed across to Tinicum Island. As he pulled his boat up on the beach a friendly voice called, "Hello!"

Lars turned around. Standing not far from the water was a girl about his own size with long yellow braids tied with blue ribbons.

"Who are you?" she asked, staring at him with wide blue eyes.

"Lars Svensen. I came over to bring Bjorn some watermelon seeds. He's the governor's farmer."

The girl took a few steps to the edge of the water.

"I know. I'm the governor's daughter—that is, one of them."

"I thought you were," Lars said. "I've heard

about your family. I've seen your father many times when he comes over to speak to us at meetings. You never come with him, do you?"

"No. I'm not allowed to. I'm never allowed to go anywhere. My father says I'm too little. But I'm eleven. How old are you, Lars?"

"Twelve."

"Well I'll soon be twelve. Everyone in the family calls me Lila. That means Little One." She frowned. "They don't think I'm big enough to even go out in the boat alone. They would *never* let me row across the river by myself."

"They don't want anything to happen to you," Lars said.

"Nothing happens to *you*," she snapped. Tears of anger filled her blue eyes. "You don't have to stay on an old island where you don't have any friends. You don't know how lonesome it is here."

"I guess that would be rough," Lars said thoughtfully. "But I'd like to be your friend."

Lila pouted. "You live too far away. Everybody lives too far away." Then her eyes brightened. "Well, I *do* have one friend. He's still awfully little. He's a puppy. My father had him sent over from Sweden. He was on the SWAN when it docked at Fort Christina last month. Would you like to see him? He's in the kitchen."

"Sure." As they walked up to the house Lars said, "I wish I had a dog. You see how lucky you are. We only have a goat. But if we didn't have her we wouldn't have any milk. Maybe later I'll have a puppy."

PRINTZHOF was surrounded by orchards. The peach trees were beginning to show pink with blossoms. In the garden a man was digging around the daffodils and shrubs that edged the path to the house. The front door opened into a hall with a large room at the side. Lars had never seen such elegance. Fine carved chairs stood against the walls. Silver bowls and candlesticks were on the tables and beautiful blue and white plates lined the shelves of the cupboards. He stood looking with his mouth and eyes wide open.

"Come on, Lars. I thought you wanted to see my puppy," Lila said.

The puppy's box was in the kitchen between two brick ovens. As soon as he heard Lila's voice he stood on his hind legs and looked over the edge, squealing happily. Lars knelt down to pat him.

"He's so white and curly," he said. "And he *is* small."

"I've named him Grendle."

"Grendle!" laughed Lars. "Do you know who Grendle was?"

"No." Lila answered. "I just liked the name."

"Grendle was an ugly monster that went around raiding towns and destroying whole armies. He was finally killed by a brave Swede named Beowulf. This little puppy shouldn't have the same name as that *monster*."

Lila thought a minute. "You're right," she said. "I'll change his name to Beowulf." She put her face close to the box and the puppy licked her nose. "Yes, from now on you're Beowulf. How do you like your new name?"

Beowulf wagged his tail.

"When you get bigger, you must protect Lila from danger just the way brave Beowulf protected his people long ago," Lars said. He patted the puppy. "When do you take him out of the box?" he asked.

"I walk him in the orchard every morning and afternoon. But when I take him in the garden he likes to chew my mother's daffodils. She gets very angry and says he must stay inside. I'm supposed to gather some flowers this morning for the table. I had better get them now. My mother will be unhappy if they aren't in her favorite bowl when she gets back."

"Where is she?" Lars asked.

"She and my sisters rowed over to Fort Christina to see about the work on the new church being built there. My father is going to give them glass for the windows."

"I never see you in church on Sundays," Lars said.

"No." Lila frowned. "My father makes us go to the chapel here. I miss all the fun. You row across to Fort Christina every Sunday and have picnics after the service, don't you?"

"Yes," Lars said. "We meet our friends and have a great time. Maybe the governor would let you come with us if we stopped some Sunday."

"Oh Lars, I don't think he would. He doesn't want us to become too friendly with the colonists.

He thinks we're just a bit better than other people in New Sweden. But I don't. I wish I had some friends like you."

As Lars scratched the puppy's ears he thought how lonely it must be here on the island with only Beowulf to play with. "Well, we can be friends, even though I do live so far away," he said. "But right now you better gather those daffodils. And I better find Bjorn and give him these seeds."

Bjorn was plowing the governor's field, getting ready to plant beans. He stopped when he saw Lars.

"Here Bjorn," Lars said, giving him the large seeds. "My father says these are special. An Indian friend gave them to him last fall. They will grow into plants with fruits this big," and he stretched out his arms touching his fingers in front. "They're called watermelon. They're really sweet."

"Thank you, Lars Svensen. And thank your father for me. I'll plant them right away."

Lars started back to the boat. Lila was in the garden picking flowers. "Goodbye," he called as he pushed the dugout into the water.

She stood up and waved.

All afternoon Lars helped his father in the field. He thought of curly little Beowulf and pretty Lila with the yellow braids and blue ribbons. Somehow they seemed just right for each other.

That night after the Svensens had gone to bed they were awakened by a gun shot. Then another. They smelled smoke. Father jumped up and ran to the window.

"Lars!" he called. "Lars, get dressed quickly.

PRINTZHOF is on fire. We must row over and help them!''

Mother and Ingrid were up now. They could see the fire leaping high in the sky over on the island. It looked as though the sauna were in flames.

Lars pulled on his shirt and breeches, slipped his feet into his moccasins and climbed down the ladder. He was still buttoning his shirt as he ran to the river.

"Here, take our bucket," Mother called hurrying after them. Lars grabbed it from her and jumped into the dugout just as his father pushed off.

It didn't take long to row to Tinicum Island. Other men from New Sweden and Fort Christina were arriving with buckets, and pulling their skiffs up on dry land.

Flames were now licking the main part of the house. Servants had carried out furniture and had set it on the lawn. There on a table piled high with clothing and pots and pans was the silver bowl containing Lila's daffodils.

The four older Printz daughters were sitting on a bench crying. Madam Printz was trying to comfort each one. Lila stood beside them in her bare feet with a blue cloak around her shoulders, horror on her face. The governor was shouting orders to his servants and to the colonists as they arrived.

The fire was spreading fast. Lars filled his bucket in the river, but as he ran, the water sloshed out wetting his shirt.

"See if you can find more buckets," his father called. "Maybe up by the barn."

Buckets were being passed in a steady line from one man to the next. They were emptied on the fire and returned to the river to be filled again. The men worked quickly but the flames kept leaping higher. Governor Printz kept shouting, "Faster men! Faster! Try to move faster!"

Lars started to the barn when someone called, "Lars!"

He stopped. Lila ran to him. Tears were spilling down her cheeks. "Lars, Beowulf's in the kitchen. My mother won't let me get him."

"You're sure he's still there?"

"Yes. You know he can't get out of his box," she sobbed.

Lars ran to the house. Flames had made their way into the hall and smoke billowed out through the huge open door. He stood there a moment thinking. Then he pulled his wet shirt over his mouth and nose and dashed inside.

"Don't go in there!" Madam Printz shouted.

Lars didn't hear her. He made his way through the hall to the kitchen. He could hear the sizzling tar in the timbers as the fire reached out across the ceiling. Then, right above the ovens, one of the wooden beams crackled and started to fall. Quickly Lars snatched the puppy from the box just as it crashed to the floor. He covered the puppy with his wet shirt and made his way to the front door and into the garden. There he took a deep breath.

Lila ran to him. Carefully he unwrapped Beowulf and put him in the little girl's arms. The puppy gave her hand a feeble lick.

"Oh Lars, thank you," she sobbed. "What would I have done if you hadn't saved Beowulf?"

"He'll be all right now," Lars said a bit shakily.

"I know he will," and she snuggled her face down into the soft thick fur.

Madam Printz strode over to Lars and shook her finger under his nose. "You were such a foolish boy to do that," she scolded. Then she smiled, and putting her arm around him she added, "And such a brave boy." She took a lace handkerchief from the pocket of her skirt and wiped the soot from his face. "Here, sit down for a while," she said as she pulled him toward a bench.

"That's all right, ma'am," Lars said feeling a bit embarrassed, "it wasn't anything. I'm glad Beowulf is safe. I better go back and help the men now," and he broke away from her strong arms.

"You're a brave boy, Lars Svensen," she repeated as she put her handkerchief back in her pocket.

All night long they battled the flames, but they couldn't save the beautiful house. As the sun came up over the South River, PRINTZHOF was nothing but smoldering ashes. Only the dairy and the farmers' houses beyond the orchard were saved.

The men got in their dugouts and skiffs to row home. Governor Printz stood on the river bank, his clothes and face blackened by smoke, his shaggy blonde hair falling on his broad shoulders.

"Thank you, men," he shouted. "Tomorrow we'll start rebuilding PRINTZHOF. I'm counting on all of you to help!"

As Lars stepped into his father's boat, Madam Printz walked down to the water's edge. "Lars Svensen," she called, "if you would care to come too, you would be welcome company at PRINTZHOF."

All heads turned toward the governor. Scowling, Johan Printz looked first at his wife, then at Lila, who was anxiously clutching Beowulf in her arms, and finally at Lars, standing in the boat. His eyes began to twinkle, and he nodded his head once or twice.

"Ya, Lars Svensen," his voice boomed over the water. "You come too."

Guns on Reed's Beach

Charity held her black stockings and her black buttoned shoes in one hand. With the other hand she lifted her grey skirt and petticoat high enough to keep them dry as she walked in ankle deep water at the edge of the bay. It felt cool to wiggle her toes in the soft sand. It felt cool, too, to have her long braids wound around her head and fastened with Mother's bone hairpins. She was only allowed to wear it this way on very hot days. She wished she had a little red bow fastened in her hair, but "Quakers don't approve of such show," her mother had told her.

As Charity poked along the beach she saw the Cope twins, seven year old Seth and Samuel marching toward her. Each one had a short pole over his shoulder that looked as though it may have been the branch of a small tree. They too were barefoot. They giggled as they kicked up the water and splashed each other.

"Hello there, are you going fishing?" Charity asked as the boys came close. "I see you have your fishing poles."

"They're not fishing poles," Seth said, a bit annoyed at her ignorance.

Charity laughed. "Of course they aren't. Let me see, they are—they are—"

"They're guns," Samuel said impatiently.

"Guns?" Charity didn't expect that answer.

"Yes. Like the British sailors carry. We're going to shoot them if they take any more of our chickens."

The little tow-heads wrinkled their noses as they looked up in Charity's brown eyes.

She patted Samuel's rumpled hair. "Now boys, thee know it isn't right to use guns to shoot anyone—even British sailors."

Seth smiled. "Well, they're just pretend guns. They don't really shoot." He took his pole from his shoulder and showed it to Charity. "It's all right to pretend, isn't it?"

Charity frowned as she wondered how to answer him. "I suppose so," she said doubtfully.

"We won't shoot anybody 'less they take our chickens," Samuel promised.

Seth shouldered his gun again and together the twins ran down the beach.

Charity sat down where the sand was dry and watched them splashing through the water. She thought how lucky it was that they had each other to play with. There weren't many children living at Reed's Beach. And no one else twelve years old for her to be friends with.

She picked up a shell and started to write her name in the sand when a ship coming up the bay caught her attention. She squinted to see it better. It was flying the British flag.

"I *hope* they don't stop here," Charity said aloud. "I *hope* they don't take any more of our food."

Even before President Madison had declared war with Britain in June, 1812, English ships had come in to Reed's Beach where sailors refilled their casks with good fresh water. The Quakers

were very glad to share this with them. But since
the war, the sailors had been raiding farms, carrying off vegetables, chickens and even cattle.

Charity wiped her sandy feet on her petticoat,
quickly put on her shoes and stockings and ran
up the road. Before she reached her house she
heard her father in the garden pounding bean
poles in the soft earth with his maul. She knew
her grandfather would be holding each pole
steady so it would stand secure for the plants
to climb. Each spring the poles were placed in
lines as straight as the line of poplar trees that
led up to their front porch. In fact, everything
about this Quaker settlement was laid out in
straight lines—the streets, the gardens, the farms,
the houses.

"Father," Charity called running up between
the rows of beans. "Father, a British ship is sailing
up the bay."

He stopped his work and leaned on the maul. A
frown crossed his face. Grandfather straightened
up and took off his wide brimmed Quaker hat,
letting the sun shine on his long white hair.

"Does thee suppose they're coming to take our
food again?" Charity asked breathlessly.

"I hope not. We'll have to wait and see,"
Father said.

"Sounds like more bad business," Grandfather
muttered.

"Well it's getting serious now. It's becoming a
regular thing," Father said.

The farmers could somehow make out if their crops were taken, but not their livestock.

"Let's go see if the ship is docking here. Maybe it's a merchant ship on its way to Philadelphia," Father suggested.

"That I doubt," Grandfather said. "Not if it's flying the British flag."

The three of them walked down the road to a little hill. To the left of the hill a wharf had been built several years ago. Often ships from England, France and other European countries had unloaded goods here that were to be sent overland. But that was before the war. Now American ports were closed to British ships. If this one stopped here today it would be for no good.

"Father, why do we let them take our things this way?" Charity asked. "Thee has said it's wrong to steal. They're stealing, aren't they?"

"Yes, Charity. And thee has given me a hard question to answer. It is also wrong to take up arms against another person. That is our strong Quaker conviction. We can't fight these sailors. Yet, neither can we allow them to carry off our food and cattle. Somehow we must find a peaceful way to prevent this."

"But how?" Charity persisted.

"That I don't know. We must trust that someone will think of a way," he said.

As they feared, the frigate ENTERPRISE had tied up at the wharf. They watched as the sailors unloaded water casks. They rolled them up the road to the spring. After filling them with the clear fresh water, they rolled them back again and stacked them on the frigate.

"I hope that's all they want. Maybe they'll leave now," Father said.

Several other villagers had seen the ship and had come to the hill to watch whatever might be going on.

"This doesn't look good," one of the men said to Father. "In the daylight they take our water. Who knows what they will take tonight."

All afternoon the ENTERPRISE swayed gently at anchor. All afternoon the men from Reed's Beach left their work to walk to the wharf and get a better view of the ship. On their way home they stopped at neighbors' homes to talk about it. They all feared another raid during the night.

By dinner time nearly everyone in the village had been down to the wharf. All was quiet on board the ENTERPRISE. Occasionally, a few sailors were seen lounging on deck. When Charity went back with her grandfather early in the evening, one of the sailors waved to her.

"Shall I wave back, Grandfather?" she asked.

'Yes, it will do no harm," he said wearily. "Perhaps thee reminds him of a little girl he has at home."

Timidly Charity raised her hand. "But Grandfather, why should we be friendly with men who steal from us?" she asked.

His troubled eyes looked down at his granddaughter's upturned face. "I'm sure they wouldn't be stealing from us if it weren't for the war," he said shaking his head sadly. "War makes men do bad things."

That evening everyone in the village gathered their cows into the barns and shooed the chickens into their coops. There were no locks on the doors. Everyone at Reed's Beach was honest and respected one another's property, so why was it necessary to have locks? But candles and kerosene lamps were kept burning in their homes far into the night.

It was very, very late when Charity's parents and grandfather went to bed. They thought she was asleep, but she lay there wide awake long after they had blown out the lamps and had stopped talking.

All was quiet when suddenly she heard footsteps outside, running up the path below her bedroom. Quickly she got up and tiptoed to the window. It was so dark and still. As the moon began to peek out from behind a cloud, she could see figures moving about down by the barn. When the moonlight became brighter she made out the forms of two of the sailors tying ropes around their cows' necks. They led them down the path to the road.

Charity stole into her parents' room. Gently shaking her father she whispered, "Father, they're taking our cows. I saw them. They just went down the path leading Clover and Bossy away,"

Father jumped out of bed. Already Mother was up and lighting candles. Grandfather was up too, and he and Father were pulling on their trousers and shirts.

They all went out on the front porch. The moon had again hidden behind clouds and it was too dark to see anything except lights flickering in houses up the road. Apparently their neighbors had also been awakened.

"What are we going to do, Father?" Charity asked angrily. "Thee can't let them walk off with Clover and Bossy."

"I hope that's all they walk off with," her father said sadly. "Sometimes it makes me wish I could take a gun against them."

"Surely we'll find a better way," Mother said. "If thee were to use a gun, thee might take a life, and that would be wrong."

"Well, there's nothing we can do tonight. But tomorrow we must set a time for a meeting to work out a plan," Grandfather said.

Quickly and quietly the men on the ENTERPRISE had made their raid. With a good supply of food on board, they pulled up anchor and sailed down the bay to the ocean. By dawn, not a trace of the ship was to be seen.

The town had suffered badly. Families who had worked hard to provide for the winter months found their supply of food gone from their barns where it had been stored. Chickens were stolen from many farms, and besides Clover and Bossy, cows had been taken from other families.

It was decided that plans to prevent more of this

activity would be discussed after First Day service. Everyone from miles around came out on Sunday. Charity, dressed in her brown First Day dress and bonnet, was glad the British hadn't taken their horse.

"What do folks do who have no horse and carriage to ride to meeting?" she asked her grandfather.

"I can easily remember times like that," he said. "We held meetings in each others' homes. That was when your father was a little fellow."

"About my age?" she asked.

"Just about," Grandfather smiled.

At the meetinghouse Charity sat on one side of the room with her mother and the rest of the women. Father and Grandfather, in their black collarless coats, took their places on the facing bench. The rest of the men sat on the other side of the room. Most of the folks were neighbors, but some had come from as far as Sluice Creek.

As she looked down the row of women in their long drab dresses of brown, grey and black, Charity thought they all looked alike. "And the bonnets tied under their chins are all the same," she said to herself. She pictured a red ribbon on her bonnet. The thought made her chuckle. Her mother gave a warning glance and put her hand on Charity's knee.

Charity stopped smiling. She knew she should be thinking pious thoughts. But it was hard to do. And Father had said this would be a long meeting.

It went on for over an hour with long periods of

silence. She tried hard to think of her sins, but the sun shone through the windows, making shadows of leaves dance on the floor. Outside, birds were singing in every tree. Her thoughts wandered off to the cool waters in the bay. She imagined how the soft sand would feel as she again wiggled her toes in it.

Suddenly Grandfather was standing in his place at the facing bench. His voice boomed through the quiet gathering.

"Friends, many of us have lost much of our food these past few months. Some have lost cattle during raids on our farms. We are glad to supply anyone with water. We are glad to share our food with the hungry. But things have gotten completely out of hand. Last week was the third raid on Reed's Beach. We cannot take up arms against the enemy. The British know this and are taking advantage of it. But they must be stopped. Thee all must have feelings on the matter. What shall we do?"

His question seemed to echo off the walls as his grey eyes searched for an answer from the men in front of him. He took his seat again on the facing bench.

At last one of the men stood up and said, "This is a problem we cannot solve now. Let us go home and consider it carefully. When we return on Fourth Day, let us hope we have an answer."

After silent prayers the meeting was over.

Dinner was usually a happy time. Everyone, including Charity, was expected to contribute to the conversation. Today everyone was quiet. Father and Grandfather were trying to think of a peaceful way to stop the British raids. Charity was thinking her own thoughts, wishing it weren't Sunday so she could go wading in the bay. She thought of the little Cope twins and how they loved to play along the water's edge. She thought of the day she saw them with their "pretend guns." Her eyes lighted up. "Father! Grandfather!" she burst out so loud she even startled herself. Mother was so surprised she dropped her fork. "Why don't we have 'pretend guns'? We could even have 'pretend cannon'."

Father looked puzzled. "What on earth is thee talking about? What does thee mean—'pretend cannon'?"

"Well, thee knows the little hill just opposite the wharf? Thee knows that beach plums and sea grass and all kinds of underbrush grow there."

"Of course."

"Why couldn't some logs be painted to look like cannon and hidden there with only their ends showing?"

"Thee means the mouths of the cannon," Grandfather said.

"Yes, with only the mouths of the cannon showing," Charity repeated.

Father thought a minute, then a broad smile spread across his face. "I think Charity has a good idea," he said. "Yes, I think it's something worth seriously considering."

"But where would thee get the logs? And how would thee strip the bark so they could be painted?" Mother asked doubtfully.

"Surely that can be worked out," Father said. "At least we have an idea to start with."

"Wouldn't Mr. Douglass be able to help?" Charity suggested. "He's a ship's carpenter. I should think he'd have lots of logs that could be painted to look like cannon."

"Charity, thee has a bright head on those shoulders," Grandfather said, a merry look in his clear grey eyes. "But where on earth did thee ever get that idea?"

Charity told how the little Cope twins had been pretending their sticks were guns and how they were going to pretend to fight the British raiders. "I guess I just thought of bigger guns—like cannon."

That afternoon Father and Grandfather went around Reed's Beach asking neighbors how they felt about the idea of the Quaker cannon. Everyone agreed that it might work. They were anxious to present it at the meeting.

A concerned group of Friends attended Fourth Day meeting that week. Everyone seemed to think they had a good plan, and they were anxious to help with the preparations.

The next few days were busy ones. Several men rode over to Sluice Creek where Mr. Douglass had his carpenter's shop and helped paint the "cannon." Others loaded them on their wagons and brought them to Reed's Beach, placing them in strategic positions on the little hill.

"How shall we sound the alarm when the next British ship sails up the bay?" one of the men asked, as they stood looking into the mouths of their cannon peeping menacingly from the underbrush.

Grandfather was ready with an answer. "The first one to see it approaching must get on his horse and ride through the village to alert us. Doesn't that seem the best way?"

They all agreed this would be an easy plan to carry out. "If only it works," Father said after dinner that night, as they discussed the cannon again.

"Oh, I hope it does," Charity said.

"I think it will," Grandfather said, as he sat down on the couch beside his granddaughter and put his arm around her. "But if it doesn't work, remember, Charity, thee was the only one who came up with an idea."

The Friends on Reed's Beach dreaded another raid, but they were anxious to see if their Quaker guns looked real enough to make the British fear them. Would these brave English sailors be too frightened to come in for food?

They didn't have long to wait. Thursday afternoon of the following week the VIXEN sailed up the bay. The first person to see it was the twins' father, George Cope. He mounted his horse and rode through the village shouting the alarm. Men stopped their work and ran to the hill. There they manned their "cannon."

The ship moved quietly through the water. When

it neared Reed's Beach it turned and headed toward the wharf. The village "soldiers" waited
breathlessly as they watched it come closer and
closer. It slowed down as it approached. All at
once there was a scurry on deck. Sailors ran to the
bow to look over at the hill. Someone on board
began shouting orders. Other sailors were shouting too, but the wind blew their words away. The
Quakers couldn't hear what they were saying.

Then the VIXEN backed water, turned and sailed
back down the bay. The men on the hill waited
until it was well on its way. Then they shouted
and waved their arms and happily slapped one
another across the back. Their guns had been suc-
cessful! They had fooled the enemy!

Everyone for miles around attended First Day
service the next Sunday, to give thanks that the
men of Reed's Beach had outwitted the British and
saved their food and cattle.

Grandfather took his place on the facing bench.
His white hair shone as the morning sun fell across
it. Everything was very quiet when he stood up
and looked at the men and women sitting in front
of him. In his booming voice he announced, "For
those of you who haven't heard, it was my granddaughter Charity, who gave us the idea for our
Quaker 'guns'." He beamed at the little girl as he
took his seat again.

Everyone turned to look at her. They smiled or
nodded. Then they went on with their service.

Charity sat very still beside her mother, watching the shadows of the leaves dance on the floor. She thought how her grandfather always made her feel happy. Today he also made her feel very proud. She knew she shouldn't be thinking of these things—not now—at First Day meeting. And she mustn't think how pretty that red bow would look on her bonnet, or about wiggling her toes in the cool wet sand. She must keep her mind on pious thoughts. But today she found it especially hard to do.

The Pied Piper of Log Gaol

There was a jovial mood at the Tavern tonight. It looked as though practically all the men of Log Gaol were crowded here on the porch to hear the Old Pig Drover tell his wonderful stories.

Joel was wedged in on the top step beside Mr. Rankin. He looked around. He was the only eleven-year-old boy here. His face glistened with a freshly scrubbed look. His unruly black hair was slicked down with water. His brown eyes danced with excitement.

"When do you suppose the Drover will be here?" Joel asked.

"When he's finished his supper," Mr. Rankin said. "Remember, he's walked those pigs more than twenty miles today. He needs a good square meal."

Mr. Rankin was the school master. Last fall he had come through New Jersey from Greenville, Tennessee on his way to Yale University. When he found that they needed a teacher at Log Gaol, he decided to stay for a few terms and earn some much needed money for his college tuition.

Joel was the oldest boy in the little one room school. He was almost as tall as Mr. Rankin, but he was thin and dark. Mr. Rankin was stocky and his hair was the color of barley growing in the fields. They had become good friends. Joel had even borrowed some of Mr. Rankin's leather-bound books about rocks and minerals.

Mr. Rankin had asked Joel's mother if he could take the boy to the Tavern tonight to hear the Drover's marvelous tales.

"Joel won't have many opportunities to hear stories like these," he had told her. And she'd said he could go.

Joel was feeling very important sitting here with all of these grown men, when Clem came up to the porch. He swung himself over the rail. Right away he spotted Joel.

"Hey Joel, how come your ma let you out tonight? The Drover ain't going to tell any little kid's stories."

The men around him laughed. Joel could feel his face getting red—even his ears.

Clem was a tall boy. Taller than Mr. Rankin. He was several years older than Joel. He had given all the teachers a hard time. Then one day shortly after Mr. Rankin became school master, Clem appeared with a black eye. No one knew for sure, but they all suspected Mr. Rankin had given it to him. The next day, Clem dropped out of school.

"I'll be glad when I'm big as he is," Joel mumbled.

"Don't let him heckle you. Just sit tight," the teacher said. "Look Joel, there's the Drover now, paying his bill at the desk."

The Pig Drover came through Log Gaol every three months, driving his shoats from Pennsylvania to market in Newark and Elizabethtown. He always stopped at the Tavern on Allemuchy Road. After leaving his pigs in the meadow behind the inn, he went up to the garret and changed his dirty clothes to clean ones. The tavern keeper gave him a good meal. The Drover always paid for his food, and the innkeeper always made money the night the Drover was there, because men came from all around the countryside to listen to his stories and buy refreshments. When the weather was cold they stayed in the big room by the fireplace. This was where all the town meetings were held. When it was warm, as it was tonight, the Drover appeared on the porch.

The crowd became quiet, as a kitchen boy lighted the oil lamp that hung from the porch rafters.

"Here he comes now!" Joel exclaimed, forgetting himself and poking Mr. Rankin in the ribs so hard he almost knocked him off the step.

The Drover stood in the doorway a moment looking over the crowd. His large frame filled the whole space. His thick grey hair was brushed back away from his face and fell around his shoulders. His blue eyes matched the color of his faded shirt, and little crinkles formed around them as he stood there smiling. He strode over to the porch rail, leaned against one of the posts and folded his arms.

"Did I ever tell you about the time I met Patrick Henry?" His voice rumbled through the night air. "He was the greatest statesman our country ever had. Yes sir!"

Joel's muscles were bunched in excitement as the Drover delivered one of Mr. Henry's speeches. He felt a magic as he watched him standing as straight as a corn stalk with the light from the oil lamp casting his long shadow on the path below. At the end of the speech the Drover thundered, "But as for me, give me liberty or give me death!"

All was quiet for a moment. Then the men stamped their feet and shouted, "More! More!"

The Drover raised his arms for silence. He told many stories. Some were funny. Some were scarey. Some even brought tears to the eyes of the men. Finally he asked, "Have you heard about the castle that was built on the top of a mountain down in Virginia?" His voice became mysterious. "Well, one night it began to crumble away. The next morning it had disappeared. Even where the highest turret had stood, there was nothing but a pile of sand and rock."

By now the moon was high in the sky. The Drover moved away from the porch railing. "That's enough for tonight," he said. "The next time I come by, I'll tell you why the castle disappeared."

He went inside and up the narrow steps to the garret.

"Come on Joel," Mr. Rankin said. "I'll walk you home."

"You don't need to do that," Joel said.

"I sure do. I told your mother I'd be responsible for you."

Joel was quiet walking along Allemuchy Road thinking of the wonderful tales he had heard. When they started up Dark of the Moon Road he asked Mr. Rankin, "What do you suppose made that castle disappear?"

"Well Joel, there may be several scientific reasons. I guess we'll just have to wait until the Drover comes to Log Gaol the next time to find out the real one."

They came to Dark of the Moon Graveyard. The tombstones stood out in the shadows looking like an army of small white ghosts all lined up for parade.

"Let's not take the short cut through the graveyard," Joel said. "Let's take the path around the church."

"Not afraid?" Mr. Rankin suggested.

"Oh no, sir. It's just that. . ."

"I know. I'd rather stick to the path tonight too."

A short distance more and they reached Joel's house.

"I'll see you in the morning," the school master said.

"Golly, thanks. Tonight sure was great," and Joel ran up the steps and inside.

Early the next morning the Old Drover called his pigs from the meadow behind the inn. They came running from all directions, crowding around him. He counted them. Twenty-nine.

"Now where is that thirtieth one?" he asked.

He called again. Down at the far end of the meadow the littlest one came bouncing out of the tall grass.

"Why are you always my problem?" the Drover chuckled, as they started up the Allemuchy Road on their journey toward Newark.

Every so often the Drover would reach into a

burlap sack he had slung across his shoulder, take out a handful of shelled corn and drop it along the way. The pigs ate it, one kernel at a time, running beside him or tagging along behind. But they never strayed away. The farmers he passed said that there was a kind of witchery in the way he drove his pigs. But the Drover said it was food and love that made them stay with him.

From then on, Joel went to the Tavern with Mr. Rankin every time the Drover was in town. They heard stories about soldiers being hidden in secret passageways during the Revolution. They had a first-hand account of the War of 1812. The Drover told about a whole family of slaves that he had bought at auction. He always ended the evening by saying, "That's all for tonight. I'll see you when I come next time."

Mr. Rankin lived at the Tavern. Often he and the Drover would sit on the porch and talk after the crowd had left—just the two of them. Once in a while, if it weren't too late, Joel would stay to listen. But the Drover never told any of his stories then. They talked about Log Gaol and about the farmers who lived near by, and about his pigs. He didn't mention his family, or what he had done when he was a boy.

One night the three of them were sitting there rocking when Joel said, "Drover, you never told us the end of the story about the castle that crumbled away."

"That's right," the Drover answered, crinkles

forming around his blue eyes. "I never did finish it, did I? Well, next time I come to Log Gaol I'll start with that one. It's too long to tell you now. But it's all true. I've been to the place where the castle stood, and there's nothing there but a pile of sand."

The next morning Joel walked slowly down Allemuchy Road on his way to school. The leather strap over his shoulder held his slate and one of Mr. Rankin's books. Just as the school bell rang he saw Clem coming down the other side of the road.

"Hi, Joel," he called. "Why don't you knock off school today and come out to the Devil's Kitchen with me?"

This was a cave not far from Log Gaol where Joel sometimes discovered interesting rocks.

"I found part of a skeleton there yesterday," Clem said, crossing the road and walking beside him. "I'm going to see if I can find the rest of him today."

"A skeleton?" Joel asked in surprise. "What of, a dog?"

"No stupid," Clem said in disgust. "An Indian."

"Whee-e-e!" Joel exclaimed. "How do you know it's an Indian?"

Clem's eyes became tiny slits as he looked at Joel. "Oh, I can tell these things."

After Joel thought a minute he said, "Clem, I don't believe you."

"Didn't think you would," Clem sneered. "Well kid, you go on to school and see your teacher friend. But remember, I gave you a chance to find something better than the rocks you're always hunting."

As Joel started across the road to the school yard, Clem yanked the strap from his shoulder. The slate flew in one direction, Mr. Rankin's leather bound book in another. Clem thrust his hands in the pockets of his jeans and started to laugh. Joel picked up the book, carefully dusted it off and quickly leafed through the pages. Fortunately it wasn't torn. Still laughing, Clem swaggered down the road.

Joel gathered up the slate and strap and ran to school. He slid into his seat in the back of the room. Opening exercises were over. Mr. Rankin had given reading to the older children and put some arithmetic on the board for the younger ones to work on.

Then he said, "Joel, would you please come here. I'd like a few words with you."

"Oh boy, here it comes," Joel thought. "If only I hadn't stopped to talk to Clem. It always happens. I get in trouble."

Mr. Rankin pulled a chair to the side of his desk.

"Sit down," he said looking very serious. "I have something to talk over with you. But first, tell me, how are you and Clem getting along?"

"Oh, all right sir." Joel looked down at the floor.

"You don't let him annoy you?"

"Not really, Mr. Rankin."

"Good boy. I saw the two of you across the road a

few minutes ago. I'll wager he tossed your things in the dust because you wouldn't do something he wanted you to do."

"Yes sir."

"Would you like to tell me about it?"

"He wanted me to go to the Devil's Kitchen and look for skeletons. He said he found one of an Indian."

Mr. Rankin laughed. "That area has been so thoroughly combed. I don't believe he'll even find an Indian arrowhead. At any rate, I'm glad you came to school. It may be hard to realize *now*, Joel, but in the long run it pays to do the right thing. Clem would be much better off if he had stayed in school and behaved himself."

"Yes sir," Joel agreed.

"But we have something more important than Clem to talk about. Last night after you left the Tavern, I sat on the porch a while longer with the Drover. Now Joel, you've heard him the last four times he's been through town."

"Five times," Joel corrected.

Mr. Rankin thought a moment. "Yes, it has been five times, hasn't it? Now tell me, has he ever repeated any of his stories?"

"No-o-o."

"Is there anything strange about them?"

Joel wrinkled his forehead while he thought. "Well, his stories are all about the South. He never tells about anything that happens up here. They're about Mississippi River steamboats, and plantations, and slaves. Even that castle that crumbled away was in Virginia.''

''You're right,'' the teacher said. ''Obviously this part of the country isn't his home. And I don't believe he is really a pig drover, either. For a long time I've had the feeling that he's a southern gentleman in disguise. Have you noticed how well he speaks?''

''Oh yes, Mr. Rankin. Like you. Do you think he went to Yale?''

Mr. Rankin laughed. ''Well I don't know about that. But something must have happened to make him live this way. For several months I've been writing letters to friends of mine in the South, asking them if they could discover anything about a man named Samuel Fulton.''

''That's the Drover's real name?'' Joel asked.

''Yes. He let that slip a few months ago when we were talking alone. But last night I asked him where in the South he had lived.''

''What did he tell you?''

''Joel, he just got up from his rocker and said, 'Goodnight, Mr. Rankin,' and went on up to the garret. I didn't see him at breakfast. That was strange, for he always gets an early start. But I knew he was still at the Tavern. His pigs were all out in the meadow.''

''Golly!'' was all Joel could say.

Mr. Rankin continued. ''This morning I found out something most interesting. I stopped at the post office on my way to school. A letter was there from his son, James Fulton. He said that his father,

Samuel Fulton, had disappeared from their home in Fayetteville, Tennessee, when he, James, was just a little boy. For years the family had tried to find him but had finally given up hope."

"Golly, why did he disappear?" Joel asked wide-eyed.

"James didn't say. But he's coming up to Log Gaol to find him. Now this is where I need your help. I want you to take James' letter to the Drover—I should say, Mr. Fulton—before he leaves the Tavern. He'll still be there. It takes him at least an hour to eat breakfast and gather his pigs together. Tell him to wait there for me. I'll be along as soon as I've answered his son's letter. I'm going to dismiss class early and post my letter on the way to the inn. You wait there too, Joel. We'll tell him everything we've found out. Hurry now."

It didn't take Joel long to reach the Tavern. And even less time to return to school.

"He's gone," he blurted out, bursting into the school room. He wiped his sweaty forehead with the sleeve of his shirt as he handed Mr. Rankin the unopened letter. "The Drover left right after you came to school. He didn't stop for breakfast and he didn't go down the Allemuchy Road the way he always goes. They said he got all his pigs together and crossed the meadow and went through the woods. He told them at the Tavern he didn't know whether he'd ever come back to Log Gaol."

"Oh no!" Mr. Rankin exclaimed. "Well, we'll have to find him."

But they didn't find him. For weeks they inquired of the farmers for miles around. No one had seen the Old Pig Drover go by. Mr. Rankin wrote to James telling him that his father had disappeared again. That he and the pigs had just vanished into nothingness.

Summer turned into fall and fall into winter, but the Drover didn't return. The men of Log Gaol missed his wonderful stories.

Then the next year, something happened that surprised everyone, especially Joel and Mr. Rankin.

It was about three o'clock one warm spring afternoon. Joel had stayed after school to look up some material on fossils. Mr. Rankin was at his desk preparing the next day's work. Two well dressed gentlemen carrying brightly colored carpet bags came into the schoolroom. One gentleman was short and stocky, the other was tall and lean. The tall one took off his high silk hat. His gray hair was brushed back and reached to his shoulders. He had the bluest eyes, and when he smiled, little crinkle lines showed around them. He just stood there looking from teacher to pupil.

Joel stared at the man. There was something— something—. Suddenly he shouted, "DROVER!"

"Well, Samuel Fulton," Mr. Rankin said, getting up from his desk and going to greet him.

"Just wanted to say thank you to a fellow native from Tennessee," Mr. Fulton said, grasping the teacher's hand in a warm hand shake. "And to my young friend who listened so attentively to all my tales." And he clasped Joel's hand too. Then he beckoned to his companion. "I want you to meet Mr. Buchanan, an old friend of mine from the South. He has spent the past year here in New Jersey looking for me. I'm glad he found me. Now I'm going back to Tennessee. I'm going home."

"You mean you'll never be back to Log Gaol to tell us more stories?" Joel asked.

"No, son. You've heard them all by this time, anyway."

"Oh no," Joel said. "We haven't heard why you left Tennessee, or why you became a pig drover." Then looking at the elegant way Mr. Fulton was dressed, he added, "Sir."

Mr. Fulton laughed. "Well Joel, I guess I do owe you that story." His voice became low and quiet. "You see, Mr. Buchanan and I were merchants in a city in the South. In fact we were partners. But I borrowed money. Lots of money. And I could find no way to pay it back. I knew that if I stayed in Tennessee the business would fail and Mr. Buchanan and my family would be financially ruined. I couldn't face that. I guess I was a coward. I managed to set up a fund for my wife and children. Then I left town. I thought that would be easiest for everyone. I came to New Jersey and became a pig drover. The rest you know."

"But how did Mr. Buchanan find you?" Joel asked excitedly. "How did he know you were in New Jersey?"

Mr. Fulton smiled. "It was through Mr. Rankin's letters. As soon as my son received the first one last year, Mr. Buchanan came up here to search for me. He found the Old Pig Drover working on a farm some miles north of Log Gaol.''

Mr. Buchanan interrupted. ''We tried to locate Samuel for years. Especially after the business began to prosper again. Then a newspaper was sent to us saying that he had died. So we gave up the search. But your letters, Mr. Rankin, again gave us hope of finding him.''

''For over twenty years I've been a pig drover,'' Mr. Fulton said. ''In some towns they call me 'The Pied Piper of Pigs.' '' A far away look came in his blue eyes. ''They were good pigs—almost all of them. I'm going to miss them.''

''*We're* going to miss *you*, Mr. Fulton,'' Joel said. ''And I think we should call you 'The Pied Piper of Log Gaol.' ''

Little crinkles again formed around the gentleman's eyes. ''Thank you, Joel,'' he said.

He put his carpet bag on one of the desks and opened it. There on top of his clothes was the burlap sack that carried the corn kernels he would scatter to the shoats as he walked along the highway.

''Would you like this, Joel?'' he asked, lifting it lovingly from the suitcase.

''Golly, yes sir! I sure would! Thanks.''

Mr. Fulton hung it across Joel's shoulder just the way he used to carry it.

''Well, that ends my story,'' he said as he closed the suitcase. He took a large gold watch from the pocket of his waistcoat. "We'd better be getting along. In just a few minutes the stage coach is going to pick us up right outside your schoolhouse. Goodbye, friends."

Joel and Mr. Rankin went outside to see the two gentlemen off. As they watched the stage disappear down the dusty road Joel said, "Mr. Rankin, I'm glad you found the Drover's family for him. But I'll sure miss his stories."

"Yes," the schoolmaster said, "all of us at Log Gaol will miss them. But I, too, am glad he's going home."

A puzzled look wrinkled Joel's face. "He never did tell us why that castle crumbled away. . ."

Life on the Canal

It started out as a busy day. The beginning of a canal trip was always that way, loading the barges, weighing in, going through the five locks at Trenton. But now their barge, THE KATIE, was out on open water. Fields and meadows seemed to float past them as they made their way lazily up the canal to Kingston.

Andrew sat leaning against the side of the cabin, his long legs stretched out in front of him, carving a horse. The knife slipped, making a gouge in the wood.

"Aw rats!" he exclaimed, screwing up his face in disgust.

"What's the trouble? You didn't cut off his ears, did you?" a cheery voice asked. His pretty red-cheeked mother came up the ladder from the cabin carrying a table cloth.

Andrew looked just like her. He had the same black hair and blue eyes. "Just about," he grumbled. "Oh Ma, I hope some day I can get that set of wood-carving tools. I broke the tip off the paring knife you gave me, and the blade of my penknife is too thick."

Every time THE KATIE tied up at New Brunswick, Andrew walked down the street and looked in a shop window at the tools he wanted so badly. He knew he could carve better if he had them. But the price was ten dollars. It might as well have been one hundred dollars. There was never extra money in a canaller's family to buy unnecessaries.

117

He had seen some wooden animals in another shop on the same street. He'd even talked to the man who carved them. The man wanted to see Andrew's animals. Andrew thought he'd show him the horse if he could get the ears the way they should be.

Ma shook the crumbs from the table cloth and came over to look at his work. "Oh Andrew, it's going to be beautiful," she said brushing his hair out of his eyes. "But you *do* need better tools."

"Do you think we'll ever have enough money to get them?" Andrew asked.

"Yes, Andy. You would have had them by now if the barge hadn't needed repairs. Try to be patient." She patted his suntanned cheek and went back to the stern where her husband stood straight and tall at the tiller, keeping the barge from bumping the bank of the canal.

The merry twinkle had left Ma's eyes. They usually sparkled like the sun on the canal. Pa's eyes were the same color blue, but they had a quiet far-away look like shadows along the bank.

"How I wish we could get those carving things for Andrew," she sighed. "He doesn't ask for much. Not the way most twelve-year-old boys do. He's wanted them for so long."

Pa didn't say anything but Ma knew he felt the same as she did.

She folded the table cloth and looked over at the towpath where her other son Jesse was walking the mules. He was six years older than Andrew.

His broad bare shoulders looked like bronze as the morning sun beat down upon them. A turkey feather pointed skyward from the brim of a straw hat that he wore at a rakish angle. He whistled a happy tune as he walked jauntily along the path.

Even the mules, Looie and Looella, seemed to be enjoying the morning now that they were past the noise of all the grating hinges as the lock gates swung open and closed, each time taking THE KATIE to a higher water level.

Andrew was still trying to smooth the rough spot between the horse's ears when Ma went down to the cabin to straighten things. Already a whole row of Andrew's wooden rabbits, cats, dogs and mules paraded across the window sills.

"Someday I'm going to carve a man," Andrew told them.

He had just the right piece of wood for it. He had found a log along the canal. It was almost two feet long and about ten inches across. He had stripped off the bark. There wasn't a knot in it. He had looked at it from all angles, turning it around and around.

"I know just how I'm going to start it," he said.

But right now his horse wasn't turning out the way he wanted it. His knife was so clumsy. He put them down and went back with Pa. Looking up in his father's weather seamed face he asked, "Pa, are all canallers poor?"

"Poor," Pa said in surprise. "What do you mean?"

"Oh, I don't know," Andrew answered. He often

wondered why there wasn't more money to buy some of the things they wanted.

"Why Andy," Pa said, interrupting his thoughts, "canallers are among the richest people on earth. We have clean, fresh air to breathe. Every morning we can see the sun rise and every evening watch it set. Each spring we hear the earth come alive and in the fall we see the colors change. If you're hungry you only have to throw a line over the side of the barge and in a few minutes you've caught your dinner. And Andy, at night the stars seem closer to the canal than anywhere else on earth. Remember when you were a little fellow, you thought you could pick them out of the sky?"

Andrew nodded.

"No son, canallers aren't poor. We're the richest people on earth," Pa repeated.

Andrew was quiet for a while before he answered. "I guess you're right Pa. I guess we are rich." But there were some things that didn't seem to fit into this idea. Why, if they were rich, wasn't there enough money to buy a good knife for his carving? Some things he couldn't understand at all.

Neither of them spoke for a while. Then Andrew said, "I'm glad we're carrying 'superior cargo,' Pa. I really like those fancy iron fences and lamp posts. Who are they for?"

"They're going to be used in a park somewhere in Connecticut," Pa answered. "The buyers had them made at Peter Cooper's foundry in Trenton."

"Wouldn't it be great if we could take them all

the way up there?" Andrew asked, smiling at the thought. "Can't you see Looie and Looella swimming up the Atlantic with THE KATIE in tow?"

Pa laughed. "Well that sure would be a surprise, knowing how much those two mules hate water."

Ma came up from the cabin with an apple for each of them. "I heard you talking about that beautiful iron work," she said. "I'm glad too, we're carrying 'superior cargo.' I'd hate to be carrying coal. With a breeze like this we'd have coal dust scattered all over the deck." She brushed a quick kiss across her husband's cheek. "We're lucky to have a ship-shape little barge that carries only the best products."

Andrew went back to his carving and sprawled out on the cabin roof. Looking over at Jesse plodding along the towpath behind Looie and Looella, he called, "Want to trade places with me?"

"Not a chance, boy," Jesse called back jokingly. "You go on with your carving. This is man's work."

Jesse loved his life on the canal. Some day he hoped to have his own barge and team of mules. He told Andrew about the bells he would fasten to the harness. "Brass bells," he said. "But they'd shine like gold."

Andrew liked the canal too, but he wanted to go to art school where he could learn the correct way to carve—maybe even out of marble. There was a school in Philadelphia where they taught you how. Jesse said he'd find out more about it.

Dreaming of all this, Andrew watched the green

fields on either side of the canal as they quietly moved past them. In some places the cows grazed contentedly. In other places trees bordered the path so closely that you couldn't see the farmland at all. Here shadows made the water look almost black, except for patches of gold where the sun shone through the leaves.

As they rounded a bend, Andrew saw the Giles' SEA PEDDLER coming toward them. Their barge was loaded with everything a canaller could need or want. It was a regular general store.

"Mornin' Miz Williams. Mornin' Cap'n," Mrs. Giles called.

Her deep toneless voice reminded Andrew of the horn he blew to let the lock keepers know when their barge was approaching the lock. She was much larger than Ma, and she always wore the strangest clothes. Andrew almost laughed when he saw what she had on today. Nothing matched. The frilly pink lace cap and red and black checked shirt just didn't go with the big flowered apron and purple trousers.

Mr. Giles poled his barge along the side of THE KATIE.

"What can I sell you today?" Mrs. Giles asked in her fog horn voice.

"Well I need a spool of white thread and some of that ointment I got last month. It's the best thing for mosquito bites," Ma said, as she looked across the deck of the SEA PEDDLER.

"Haven't the critters been real bad this year?" Mrs. Giles asked, clicking her tongue.

"And I need five pounds of flour and two pounds of corn meal," Ma added.

"I just got some of the prettiest material. You might like it to make new curtains for your cabin," Mrs. Giles said. She began unfolding a bolt of pale green muslin sprinkled with red geraniums. "Now wouldn't this look real pretty in your windows after that pale blue you've had hanging there so long?"

Ma's eyes beamed. "Oh, it is pretty," she said. Then a frown wrinkled her forehead. "But I hadn't intended to get material until we go back to the city for the winter. I thought I'd make new curtains while the captain and the boys were painting the barge and gettng things ready for next spring."

"You better take the material now. I know as soon as the other canal women see it they'll buy it up real fast."

Ma took a small purse from her apron pocket and counted her money. "No," she said. "I'll wait until later."

Just then, Annabelle, the little Giles' toddler, got tangled in the rope tied around her waist. She tripped and fell on the deck, letting out a howl.

"Oh dear," Mrs. Giles cried, dropping the red geranium material and running to pick up the baby. "There there, Annabelle, let your ma see what hurts." She cuddled the child in her arms.

Soon Annabelle was all smiles.

"I'll be so glad when I don't have to keep her tied," Mrs. Giles said. "But the way she's into everything it'll be a real long time till then. Still,

I'd rather pick her up here than try to fish her out of the canal.''

Ma smiled as she thought of the time she kept her two boys tethered to the cabin.

"You want the red geraniums, Miz Williams?" Mrs. Giles asked holding up the bolt of material.

"No. Not now," Ma answered.

"Too bad," Mrs. Giles said, clicking her tongue. "They'd look real pretty at those windows."

She weighed out the flour and corn meal and passed them over the side of the barge. Then she spotted Andrew.

"You still whittlin', Andy?" she bellowed.

"Yes'm."

"Let's see what you're making."

He slid off the cabin roof and handed his carving across the barge.

"That's real nice," Mrs. Giles said inspecting it carefully. "But for me—well—I like cats." Then she noticed the knife he held in his other hand. "You know Andy, you could do better if you had a good knife. Not that *that* one isn't real good," she added quickly, "but the blade's too thick."

"We know, Mrs. Giles," Ma said, paying for her purchases. "We're going to buy Andrew a set of carving tools some day."

"Well I don't have a set of tools, but I've got some real good penknives on board. Let me know if you ever want one." Then she called back to her husband, "That's all, Mr. Giles."

He stopped his conversation with Pa and pushed

the SEA PEDDLER away from THE KATIE. Soon the barges were on their way in opposite directions.

Ma took her purchases down to the cabin. She looked at her plain blue curtains. The red geraniums would look pretty at the windows, but she'd have to wait until later. . .

They were nearing Port Mercer. There Jesse would put the feed bags on Looie and Looella. Andrew would take over and guide the mules while his brother came aboard for lunch. Then Jesse would walk the towpath the rest of the way to Kingston.

Just before six o'clock they approached the Kingston lock. Andrew blew the horn, a signal that THE KATIE was close. Mr. Vanderveer, the lock tender, began turning the wheel that opened the gate for their barge.

Out on the towpath Jesse was shouting, "Whoa, whoa." Looie and Looella came to a standstill, while water in the lock was brought to the proper level. Then the far gate was opened. Jesse gave the reins a flip and the mules pulled the barge through the lock a short distance to the basin. They would tie up here for the night. Andrew helped his pa secure THE KATIE to the wharf. Jesse untethered the mules. Andrew pulled in the towline and coiled it on the deck.

"Can I go to the stable with you, Jess?" he asked as he jumped over to the wharf.

"Sure," his brother said, handing him the reins. "You can be in full charge from here on."

Andrew liked going to the stable and seeing the bargemen as they brought their mules in for the night. He liked talking with Jake, the stable boy. But tonight Jake was too busy for any conversation, except to say, "I'll take good care of Looie and Looella. They'll be brushed down and have plenty of oats to eat." He took the reins from Andrew and led the mules to their stalls.

When the boys arrived back at the barge, Ma was spooning out large portions of stew she had made of the beef and fresh vegetables she had bought in Trenton that morning.

"Let's sleep up on deck, Andy," Jesse suggested as he finished supper.

"Sure," Andrew agreed. He grabbed two blankets and followed his brother up the ladder.

"Don't talk too long," Pa said. "We want to push off at five o'clock tomorrow morning."

Andrew liked to sleep on deck. It was so peaceful and quiet watching the stars come out.

"Did you hear any stories before we left Trenton, Jess?" he asked.

Jesse chuckled. "Yes. As a matter of fact I heard one about Jonesey."

"Not another one about him!" Andrew exclaimed.

Mr. Jones, or Jonesey as he was called, was disliked by every canaller on the waterway. He drove his mules hard, trying to exceed the four mile an hour speed limit. This caused all sorts of problems. Sometimes the mules bucked and snarled the towlines of different barges. Mr. Jones always became red-faced and angry and started shouting. He shouted at the mules. He shouted at the drivers. He shouted at the bargemen. You could count on confusion when Mr. Jones was on the canal.

"Do you know what he did last week?" Jesse asked.

"No, what?"

"He was filling bottles with canal water and selling them to the gentlemen at the Red Mill Tavern for genuine spring water. He told them it would cure all kinds of aches and pains."

"Golly, I don't think that was very funny," Andrew said.

"It wasn't," his brother agreed. "The funny thing happened when the gentlemen found out what he had done. Last week Jonesey went back to the tavern with more of his spring water. He didn't expect to find the same gentlemen there. But they were waiting for him. They tossed him into the canal and threw the bottles of water in after him. It all happened so fast Mr. Jones didn't know what was going on."

Both boys started to laugh.

"Then what?" Andrew asked.

"Well, Jonesey sputtered and thrashed around, holding his head up out of the water looking like a drowned muskrat and bellowing, 'Help me, Mrs. Jones. Throw me a line!' "

Between bursts of laughter Andrew asked, "Did she?"

"Yes. But she stood leaning over the barge looking at him for a long time before she finally fished him out."

Finally their laughter changed to yawns. They pulled their blankets around them, and as they watched the stars march across the sky and listened to the water lapping against the barge, they fell asleep.

The next morning Pa was at the tiller and Jesse was walking the towpath with the mules when Andrew came down the ladder rubbing sleep from his eyes.

"After breakfast you can catch some fish for dinner," Ma said.

About the middle of the morning, Andrew was sitting with his bare feet dangling over the side of the barge. He had caught enough fish for today. He decided to work at his carving. Maybe he could fix the horse's ears. He heard Jesse command, "Haw Looella, haw. HAW!"

Pa looked over at the towpath. "What's the matter?" he called.

"It's these buttercups along the side of the path. This silly mule wants to eat them."

Jesse pulled on the reins. Looella dug her hoofs into the ground and let out a loud bray. Looie, not liking his walk interrupted in this manner, looked at her with disgust and bit her ear. At that, Looella turned full face toward the buttercups and with her hind feet, kicked her teammate. Poor Looie was startled. He backed up to the canal, lost his footing and slid into the water, pulling Looella after him. The reins were yanked out of Jesse's hand. The barge began to swing around in crazy half circles. There was a fury of kicking, braying and splashing.

In a flash Andrew dove into the canal. Being careful not to get in the way of the hoofs of the two angry mules, he grabbed the reins and swam to the bank. Jesse pulled him up on dry ground. Together they hauled the bedraggled Looie and Looella up the side of the canal and back on the towpath.

"You stupid Looella," Jesse said angrily as he tried to straighten out the harness. "That'll teach you not to eat the buttercups!"

Andrew untangled the towline. Order was once more restored. He swam back to the barge and Pa pulled him up on deck. Again THE KATIE moved quietly on her way. Andrew stretched out in the warm sunshine to dry off.

A short while after going through the Bound Brook Lock they passed Mr. Duffy, the path walker, inspecting the other side of the canal and plugging holes in the bank with sod.

"Good afternoon, Mr. Duffy," Pa called. "Finding many holes?"

"Tarnation, yes. Durned muskrats must be trying to burrow through to the Raritan River. I've filled more than two dozen today," he replied, and he went on repairing the bank.

Andrew slid off the cabin roof and went back to Pa. "It doesn't seem right to destroy their holes," he said. "They have to have a home too."

"I know," Pa answered seriously. "I've often thought the same thing. But the sides of the whole canal would cave in if we let them make their nests everywhere they wanted to."

Andrew nodded slowly in agreement. "But it still doesn't seem right." He took a big deep breath and exhaled slowly in a long sigh. "I guess it's just another one of those things I don't understand."

Pa shook his head. "I don't understand some things either, Andy." He put his arm around the boy's shoulders and they stood quietly together. Then he asked, "How's the horse coming along?"

"It's all right, I guess. But I'm not going to show it to the man in the shop this time. It isn't ready."

Pa smiled. His son wanted perfection. Already he was a good craftsman. Someday he might be a fine sculptor.

Now they had come to New Brunswick. After passing the Harbormaster and going through the locks, THE KATIE tied up in the basin. Tomorrow their beautiful iron cargo would be unloaded and sent on its overland trip to Connecticut.

The waterfront was alive with activity. Barges were arriving, mules were being unhitched. The bigger barges carrying coal and iron were being fastened together in "strings," to be towed by steam tug across the bay to New York piers.

Pa and Andrew secured THE KATIE to her little wharf and put the gangplank in place. It wasn't yet four o'clock. A good part of the afternoon was still ahead.

"Pa, may I go over and look in some shop windows?" Andrew asked.

"Not yet, Andy. I must go to the shipping office and find out what time we'll be unloaded tomorrow. When I get back you can be on your way."

"Can't I go with you now?"

"No, son. I'd like you to be here if someone should come to check the cargo."

Andrew's disappointment showed in his eyes, but he knew business had to come first.

Pa was back in a very short time. "Now be on your way," he said.

A merry heart was beating under Andrew's shirt as he stepped across the gangplank. He hurried down the street to look in the shop window at the beautiful wood carving tools gleaming in their leather case. It would be exciting to see them and know that some day they would belong to him. He could almost feel the way the sharp blades would peel through the wood.

He ran the last few steps to the shop. But when he looked in the window the set of knives was gone! Somehow Andrew had always counted on their being there, until he was able to buy them. Feeling downhearted and miserable he went inside.

"What is it, son?" the owner asked, peering over his silver rimmed spectacles.

"The wood carving set you had in the window," Andrew said slowly. "It isn't there now."

"No, son," the shopkeeper replied. "I finally

sold it. Lucky I did, too. It had been in the window several months and no one seemed to want it."

Andrew's heart felt as heavy as one of the stones in the rip-rap along the canal. "Thank you, sir," he whispered as he went out.

Slowly he started back to the wharf. He passed the carver's shop but he didn't even look in the window. At THE KATIE his mother was preparing supper. Jesse was meeting some of his friends and wouldn't be there to eat with them. Pa was tidying the deck so everything would look spanking clean when the men came down for their iron work tomorrow.

"You're back in a hurry," Pa said, as Andrew came aboard and leaned against the cabin.

"Yes, sir."

"Is everything all right?"

"Yes, sir."

Mother called up from below, "Supper's ready. And we have some fresh muffins made from Mrs. Giles' corn meal. You know they're bound to be real good," she chuckled.

"Come on, Andy. We can't keep your Ma waiting." Pa put his arm around his son's shoulder.

"I don't want any supper."

"Not want any of Ma's corn meal muffins? Of course you do," Pa said cheerfully.

Andrew wanted to stay topside alone, but he slowly followed his father down to the cabin. When he reached the bottom of the ladder and turned around, his eyes almost popped out of his head.

There in the center of the table, shining just the way they had in the shop window, were the beautiful wood carving knives elegantly resting in the brown leather case.

"Oh, Pa!" Andrew exclaimed. "Oh Pa, you were the one who bought them!"

Carefully he took them out of the box one by one. The wooden handles felt so good in the palm of his hand. Cautiously he felt the sharp blades and pointed tips. Then just as carefully he returned them to their proper grooves in the case.

"I don't think we'll need the oil lamp at the table," Ma said. "Andy's eyes are shining bright enough for us to see without it."

It was a happy Andrew who went to bed that night. Tomorrow he would use his new tools to finish the horse. Then he would begin his carving of a man. It would be a fine man, straight and tall as though he were standing at the tiller. A man just like his Pa.

The Light on Old Cape May

Susan stood at the gate with her father. A frown crossed her face as she watched her mother drive off with their horse and carriage.

"I don't see why I couldn't take Ma to Aunt Jane's," she said. "I can handle Nellie better than Ma can. She'd much rather have me hold the reins. But no. I always have to stay home."

She fought back angry tears.

"Enough of that, Susan," her father said gently. "You're twelve now and old enough to understand why you can't leave the Point today. We can't take a chance of missing the tender if it should arrive with kerosene for the light."

Susan's father was the keeper of the lighthouse on Cape May Point. Often during the day he would take summer visitors out in his boat. Today a gentleman was riding over from Cape May to go deep sea fishing with him.

Susan tossed her head. The breeze blew wisps of her short brown hair across her face. Her blue eyes flashed with anger. "I can't drive Ma to Goshen, and I can't go fishing with you and the gentleman from Virginia. I can only fool around here all day *in case* the tender comes in with kerosene. I never can do what *I* want to do."

"Susan, I don't like your tone of voice," Pa said sternly.

"I don't think you like anything I do." Susan

slammed the gate shut and started across the dunes to the lighthouse. Tears stung her eyes, and, as she plowed through the dune grass, long tendrils pricked her ankles and whipped her bare legs.

She stooped over to roll down the legs of her blue overalls. As she stood up she bumped into Tommy, practically upsetting herself. She hadn't even noticed him coming toward her.

"What's the matter, Sue?" he asked, looking at the tears trickling down her suntanned cheeks.

"Oh, nothing," she grumbled, and stumbled on.

"I only asked a question," he called.

"Well I *answered* you."

"Girls!" Tommy muttered and continued toward the beach.

Tommy was a lanky boy who lived in a shack on the bay. He didn't have any mother. His father was a fisherman who often was away at sea for several weeks at a time, leaving his son all by himself. Tommy's teeth were crooked and his yellow hair was always scraggly. And although he was only fourteen, he smoked a corncob pipe.

"Poor child! That's the way he tries to show how big and independent he is," Susan's mother said.

Tommy loved the sea. Sometimes he would climb the steps of the lighthouse with Sue and her father and just stand there looking off in the distance.

"Some day I'm going to sail all the way to Spain," he told them.

Right now Sue didn't have time to think about Tommy. She had her own problems. She pushed open the lighthouse door. There was always something comforting about coming here—something friendly about the old light. She wondered if sailors felt the same way when they saw her beam far out at sea. She was sure they must.

Round and round she climbed the spiral staircase. When she reached the gallery she stepped out on the platform and leaned against the iron railing. One hundred seventy feet below her the ocean spread like a sheet of blue-green satin. Everything looked so small down there—even the monstrous waves that crashed against the shore, leaving a fringe of white foam on the sand. In the distance she saw the sails of a ship. She wondered if it were going to Spain.

She was feeling very sorry for herself when Pa opened the gallery door, stepped out on the platform and leaned against the rail beside her.

"Susan, you spoiled a surprise I had for you," he said.

She looked up in his ruddy face. "A surprise?" she asked.

"Yes. The gentleman who is going fishing with me this afternoon is riding his horse over from Cape May. I told him how well you could handle a horse. He wondered if you would like to ride his stallion. He's a beauty. I've seen him. His name is King. I wanted to surprise you."

She bit her lip. Guilty thoughts tumbled through her head. So that was why Pa wanted her to stay home—so she could ride King. And she had thought such awful things.

"Oh Pa, I'm sorry. I didn't mean what I said.

Why do I say those things? Sometimes I hate myself!''

"No need to hate yourself. Just think before you answer so angrily. Next time, ask yourself, 'Do I really mean it?' and you probably won't say it."

Sue was quiet for a while. At last she said, "I'll try Pa. Really I will."

They stood there looking across the ocean. Then Sue put her arm around her father. "Did you really tell the gentleman from Virginia that I can handle a horse well?" she asked.

"I sure did," Pa said. "I told him that no one around here can ride as well as you can. After all, you've been responsible for Nellie ever since we've had her. You've brushed her, fed her, kept her stall clean and exercised her every day."

Susan's blue eyes sparkled. "Well she's a good horse," she said. "I love Nellie."

Pa looked at Sue, so tall and slim for her twelve years. He patted her tanned hand resting on his arm. "We better get the light ready for her work tonight before the gentleman and King arrive," he said.

They climbed a few more steps to the light room. Sue stood in the center, surrounded by the heavy glass lenses. She began polishing each section with a soft cloth. Every day she and Pa did this so that not a speck of soot would interfere with the beam as it flashed across the ocean. Pa trimmed the wicks and checked the kerosene.

When all was finished, Susan flung the cloth

over her shoulder and stood back, watching the sun make patterns on the curved glass surface.

"She sure does shine, doesn't she, Pa?"

"None shines brighter than the light on old Cape May," Pa said.

This was the third and best lighthouse that had been built on the Point. That was in 1859. The same year Susan was born.

"Pa, how many ships has the light saved from being wrecked?"

"It's hard to say, Sue. But there must have been dozens of them. You can see her beam nineteen miles out at sea."

Susan gave a final rub with the cloth to remove a smudge she had missed. Then she and Pa left the light room. Halfway down the stairs they stopped to look out the window in the side of the lighthouse.

"Nineteen miles!" Susan said. "That's farther than I can see, isn't it Pa?"

"It sure is," he answered.

"Do you suppose she ever helped pirate ships?"

"She marked the location for all ships that passed this way," Pa said. "And sure enough, some of them were pirate ships."

As they curved down the rest of the steps, Sue wondered whether there might even be some treasure buried here. Perhaps around Lily Lake. Maybe Tommy would know. She'd have to ask him.

Arm in arm, she and Pa walked back to the house. Mother had prepared a lunch before she

left for Aunt Jane's. While they were eating, Sue
asked, "Pa, this gentleman from Virginia, is he
a gambler?"

"What makes you ask a question like that?"

"Well, Ma said that many men come to Cape
May just to gamble. She said that especially the
ones from Maryland and Virginia who stay at
THE BLUE PIG sometimes lose their whole plantations playing cards."

Pa smiled. "I suppose that may be true sometimes. But I don't think this gentleman is a gambler.
He brought several horses with him to ride along
the beach. He would like to sell them while he's
here. No, I don't think he's a gambler."

Pa looked at the clock. "The tide's just about
right to start out. This gentleman has never been
deep sea fishing and he's anxious for an afternoon
on the ocean. I'll go down to the wharf and get the
boat ready. You can tell him where to find me."

Sue was standing by the gate when the gentleman galloped up on the most beautiful horse she
had ever seen. His reddish gold coat glistened in
the sunlight and his black mane and tail drifted
out behind him. Gentleman and horse came to a
quick stop when they saw her.

"Hello there. You're Miss Susan, I suppose," the
gentleman said. A smile spread over his friendly
face.

"Yes sir," she answered, returning his smile.

He dismounted, and as he stood there beside
King in his bright blue jacket, black riding breeches
and polished boots, Sue thought how elegant he

looked. But not to go fishing! Pa would never dress that way to go out in the boat. He always wore his oldest clothes.

"Your daddy is taking me deep sea fishing this afternoon," the gentleman said eagerly.

"Yes sir. He's down at the dock getting the boat ready. He said for me to tell you he'd meet you there." Going over to the horse, Sue patted his smooth neck.

"Your daddy told me you would take care of my horse. He said that you were a very good horse-woman. I thought you might like to ride King for a while. He likes to trot on the firm sand along the water's edge."

"Oh, yes sir," Susan said. Her eyes sparkled with excitement as the gentleman handed her the bridle. "I sure would like that. He's a beauty."

"He's gentle as a puppy."

"He's bigger than our mare."

"Not too big for you to manage?"

"Oh, no sir."

"Are you used to this kind of saddle?"

"Well I usually just put a blanket over Nellie's back and ride her that way."

"Hm," the gentleman said stroking his chin. "But you have used a saddle?"

"Oh yes. I can ride either way."

"You know, Miss Susan, I wouldn't go off and leave King with every stranger. But your daddy assured me you rode well and wouldn't have any problems."

King nuzzled Susan's neck.

"We won't have any problems. Don't you worry one bit. We'll make out just fine."

"Of course you will," he smiled. "I can already see that King likes you." The gentleman shortened the stirrup straps. "There," he said. "That's more your length. Now let me see you mount him."

He could tell at once that Sue knew how to handle the horse. No, he wouldn't worry one bit about either of them. "Now tell me, where will I find your daddy?" he asked.

"He's at the wharf. Right down there." Sue pointed towards the bay.

"Have a good time and take care of Miss Susan," the gentleman said, patting King's nose. He started across the dunes.

"I hope you catch some big fish," Sue called after him.

It didn't take long to become friends with King. The horse seemed to know that Susan understood him, and he responded.

The afternoon whizzed by as they trotted or galloped along the water's edge where the beach was firm. Every so often they would stop. Looking out over the ocean Sue would say, "Can you see them out there, King?" But Pa's boat was nowhere in sight.

They wandered up into softer sand and were just loping along when Tommy appeared over the dunes. He walked up beside them and took hold of the bridle. "How 'bout you let me ride him a while?" he said.

"Tommy, I can't do that."

"Why not? You think I can't handle him?"
he asked.

"No, it isn't that. It's just—well if anything
should happen to him, I'm responsible."

Tommy's lip curled back, showing his uneven
teeth. "You think nothing will happen to him
while *you're* riding him?" he taunted.

He let go of the bridle, gave King a sharp slap on
the flank and let out an unearthly yell.

Startled, King bolted across the dunes, stumbling
and kicking up the soft sand. Sue tightened the
slack in the reins and gently pulled on them.

"Whoa King! Easy King," she coaxed. But the
horse struggled until he came to firm ground. Sue
pulled on the bridle again, bringing King to a halt.
He stood trembling, his ears pointed and his nostrils
flaring in quick noisy snorts.

Susan bent forward. "It's alright boy." She patted
his sleek neck. In a few moments he relaxed.

Sue was a bit shaken too. When she was sure
King was calm she said soothingly, "I think we
better go back to the barn. We've had enough for
today. Besides, you have to take the gentleman
back to Cape May tonight."

As they crossed the dunes again, Susan saw
Tommy slowly walking towards the bay. She
couldn't decide whether to be angry at him, or
just sad.

In the barn, she unfastened the straps and lifted
off King's saddle. She brushed his coat and led
him into the mare's stall. Then she slid down in a
corner of the barn and watched him eat oats from

the mare's bucket. The sun slanted through the open door and Sue realized it was getting late. Pa should be back soon. In the meantime, she decided to wander down to the wharf—maybe go out in her own little rowboat. She'd stay close to shore, perhaps catch a few fish.

She had just thrown her lines over the side of the boat when storm clouds began gathering in the east, changing the sky to a slate grey in a matter of minutes. The steady wind had become strong gusts. The water was choppy. Her little craft bobbed up and down like a cork when a fish had her bait. Waves splashed over the side.

She drew up her lines and reached for the oars. All at once the rain pelted down in huge drops, stinging her face and arms. She pulled on the oars with all the strength she had, but the wind blew against her, carrying her steadily away from the dock. She became panicky. Then she heard a voice yell, "Sue! Hey Sue—catch!" There was Tommy standing on the dock, holding the life preserver that Pa always left there, with its yards and yards of rope fastened to it.

"Here it comes," he shouted as he threw it out across the angry water. It landed at Sue's feet. Tommy tugged on the rope and steadily towed the tiny boat in to the wharf. He reached for the chain in its bow. "I'll tie her up," he shouted above the howling wind. With expert fingers he secured it to the dock.

Sue was trembling as she climbed out of the

boat. Trembling with cold and trembling with fear. Tears mixed with the rain.

"Oh Tommy, thanks," she panted. "I'm so glad you were here. What would have happened to me if you weren't?"

They stared at one another in the beating rain. Sue sure looked bedraggled, and Tommy's wet shirt was plastered to his thin body, showing every rib.

"I guess that evens things up now. I'm sorry I tried to spook your horse," he said. Then bracing himself against the wind, he started down to his shack.

"Thanks for the rescue," Sue called through the screeching gale.

Now the storm was furious, lashing the sea and sending great waves crashing against the wharf. Sue shielded her eyes from the blinding rain and looked out over the angry sea for Pa's boat. She could see nothing but mountains of waves. Suppose his little sloop couldn't get through the storm. Suppose. . .

For a moment she thought of her mother. She was glad she was safe at Aunt Jane's. And Nellie was safe in the barn there. The mare was so afraid of storms. She thought of King. Was he afraid too? She had better go find out.

Walking against the wind it took so long to reach the barn. As she opened the door the horse whinnied.

"It's all right, King," she said, edging into the

stall and putting her arm around his neck. "They'll be home soon."

But would they? It was dark now. Almost as dark as midnight. Flashes of lightning streaked the sky and thunder rumbled in the distance. The lamp in the lighthouse should be lighted. Pa might be looking for it this very minute.

She fastened the barn door and made her way across the wet dunes. Her shirt and overalls were soaked through. And she was so cold!

It was just as dark inside the lighthouse. She groped her way to the steps and felt for the railing. Round and round she went and up, up, up she climbed in the blackness. She felt dizzy when she reached the gallery. A few more steps and she reached the light room.

She felt for the box where the matches were kept. Taking one, she struck it. It flared into a tiny yellow flame. She touched it to the wick, but the wick wasn't high enough. It wouldn't catch. The match burned her fingers and she dropped it. It went out and again all was dark. She felt for the key to turn the wick higher, then struck another match. Again it became a tiny yellow flame. This time the wick caught. Slowly the flame grew larger. One by one the other four wicks became circles of light, and the light on old Cape May threw her beacon far out across the ocean.

"If only Pa can see it," she breathed.

All at once Sue felt so tired. Her legs became rubbery and she shivered in her wet clothes. She sat down on the platform in the heat of the light. It was so warm and comforting. She put her head on her drawn up knees and softly began to cry. Then sleep took over.

The next thing she knew she was awakened by a horse whinnying.

"Nellie," she thought. "Something's happened to Nellie." Then she remembered that Nellie was at Aunt Jane's. It was King she heard.

She bounded down the stairway. As she passed the window she noticed a sky full of stars. The rain had stopped and the clouds had all blown away.

From the bottom of the stairs she saw Pa and the gentleman from Virginia talking outside the door. King was there too, saddled and ready to ride back to Cape May.

"You're a good seaman, sir," the gentleman was saying. "I don't want to repeat tonight's experience, but I must say you know how to handle your boat."

Susan rushed out the door and over to her father. "Oh Pa, I'm so glad you're home," she said trying to hold back happy tears. "I was so afraid you wouldn't find your way out of the storm."

He put his arm around his daughter. "Well Susan, we might not have made it if it hadn't been for the light. But the minute I saw her beam, I knew we'd get back safely."

King loped over and put his nose close to Susan's face. She could feel his warm breath on her cheek.

"King and I want to thank you, Miss Susan," the

gentleman said. "I had a right good adventure out there with your daddy. And I'm sure King enjoyed his afternoon with you. I'm grateful to you, young lady."

He bowed to her in a most grown-up way. Then he shook Pa's hand. "Next time we'll try to catch fish instead of a storm." He swung up in the saddle and started down the road. "But it was a great adventure. King and I will be back real soon," he called over his shoulder. Soon they had disappeared in the darkness.

Pa looked at his daughter standing there in the shadow of the lighthouse. High above her its beam was flashing out over the ocean, again guiding ships in the night. He linked her arm in his. "It's been a long day Sue. How about a sandwich and a cup of hot cocoa before we go to bed?"

"Sounds good," she said cheerily. Then she became serious. "Oh Pa, I'm so glad I stayed home today. Suppose I had gone with you and the gentleman. Suppose no one had been here to light the light."

"Let's not think of that, Sue. You *were* here, and you *did* light the light on old Cape May. And many a sailor was grateful to see its beacon tonight." Pa smiled at his daughter. "I'm so proud of you, Sue," he said. "And I'm grateful that you weren't out in the storm. It was real bad. It made me feel better just knowing that you were here, safe and warm and dry."

Sue smiled to herself. Aloud she said, "I'm

grateful too, Pa. Grateful that Tommy was here."

"Tommy?" Pa questioned.

"I'll tell you all about it when we get our cocoa," she said, as they started across the wet dunes toward the house.

Afterword

These stories are all based on fact or legend. They could be true. New Jersey's history is chock full of excitement and adventure. Surely many children must have played important parts in it all, even though their names aren't known to us. That's why I decided to give them names and tell how they might have shared in the drama of New Jersey's growth from colony to state.

The facts about the Revolutionary War are in your history books. You can even visit Tempe Wick's home in Jockey Hollow and see where her horse spent the night in the guest room.

History also tells how some New Jerseyans helped slaves on their Underground Railroad journey to freedom. It tells us about the colonies built by the Swedes along the Delaware River, and about the peaceful means the Quakers used to do brave deeds.

We know that pirates and smugglers carried on a lively business along the Jersey seashore. You can still see the lighthouse built at Cape May Point to guide ships as they sailed up the Atlantic Ocean to Delaware Bay.

And not too long ago, both the Delaware-Raritan Canal and the Morris Canal were busy waterways carrying cargo across the state from Pennsylvania to New York.

As for the ghosts that haunt some of the pages in this book. . .

Well, I'll let you decide about them.

Bibliography

Alexander, Robert Crozer, *Ho! For Cape Island*, published by the author, 1975.

Beck, Henry Charlton, *Tales and Towns of Northern New Jersey*, Rutgers University Press, 1964.

Chase, Mary Ellen, *The Story of Lighthouses*, W.W. Norton & Co., 1965.

Coles, Henry I.., *The War of 1812*, University of Chicago Press, 1971.

Collection, *A New Jersey Reader*, Rutgers University Press, 1961.

Cunningham, J. Pearson, *Cape May County Story*, Laureate Press, 1975.

Cunningham, John, *New Jersey Sampler*, N. J. Almanac Inc., 1964.

Hoffman, Robert V., *The Revolutionary Scene in New Jersey*, American Historical Company Inc., 1942.

McClellan, Robert J., *The Delaware Canal*, Rutgers University Press, 1967.

McMahon, William, *South Jersey Towns*, Rutgers University Press, 1973.

Nelson, William, *History of the New Jersey Coast,* Vol. 1, Lewis Publishing Co., 1902.

Still, William, *The Underground Railroad,* Johnson Publishing Co. Inc., 1970.

Turp, Ralph K., *West Jersey Under Four Flags,* Dorrance & Company, 1975.

Veit, Richard F., *The Old Canals of New Jersey,* New Jersey Geographical Press, 1963.

Other Middle Atlantic Press Titles
about New Jersey

Phantom of the Pines
More Tales of the Jersey Devil
by James F. McCloy & Ray Miller, Jr.
0-912608-95-1 • $12.95

The Jersey Devil
By James F. McCloy & Ray Miller, Jr.
0-912608-11-0 • $10.95

The Pine Barrens
Legends and Lore
by William McMahon
0-912608-19-6 • $9.95

Just Around the Corner in New Jersey
by Edward Brown
0-912608-17-X • $7.95

Blackbeard the Pirate
and Other Stories of the Pine Barrens
by Larona Homer
0-912608-26-9 • $9.95

George Washington's New Jersey
A Guide to the Crossroads of the American Revolution
By Craig Mitchell
0-9705804-1-X • $12.95

Published by:
Middle Atlantic Press
10 Twosome Drive • Moorestown, NJ 08057

Now Available at Your Local Book Store!